HD

St. Helens Libraries

Please return / renew this item by the last date shown.
Books may be renewed by phone and Internet.

Telephone - (01744) 676954 or 677~~les~~
Email - centrallibrary@sthel~~~~
Online - sthelens.gov.uk/lib
Twitter - twitter.com/STHLib

KU-545-084

G21 - - AUG 2015	09 - - MAY 2023	
M3 - OCT 2015		
R7 - - DEC 2015		
K9 - - APR 2016		
2 6 SEP 2016		
G18		
Q8 - - APR 2019		
Q14 - - JUL 2019		
E22		

LOVE IN A MIST

When Jill Laity inherits a cottage and some land in Cornwall, she decides to set up a garden centre with the help of her friend Judy. But tensions mount when she refuses to sell part of the land to neighbouring farmer Brandon Trelease, a widower with a young son. When Judy leaves to tend to her ailing mother, Jill struggles on her own — and then she has an accident. Bran comes to the rescue, and gradually they become close ... but can they resolve their problems?

Books by Janet Thomas
in the Linford Romance Library:

THE TIDES OF TIME
SUMMER SOJOURN
THE DANCING MAIDENS
THE OLD SUMMERHOUSE
SHADOWED LOVE
YESTERDAY'S SECRETS
CORNISH QUEST
A MIDSUMMER DREAM
PASSAGE OF TIME

JANET THOMAS

$\blacklozenge$

LOVE IN
A MIST

Complete and Unabridged

LINFORD
Leicester

First published in Great Britain in 2014

First Linford Edition
published 2015

A catalogue record for this book is available
from the British Library.

ISBN 978–1–4448–2517–6

Published by
F. A. Thorpe (Publishing)
Anstey, Leicestershire

Set by Words & Graphics Ltd.
Anstey, Leicestershire
Printed and bound in Great Britain by
T. J. International Ltd., Padstow, Cornwall

This book is printed on acid-free paper

1

'Jill! Over here!'

As I entered the coffee shop I caught sight of my best friend Judy waving furiously to catch my attention over the heads of the other customers. I raised a hand and paused while my eyes adjusted from the glare outside, then made my way over to the corner where she was keeping a place for me on a big squashy sofa.

'Oh, Jude, it's so lovely to see you!' We embraced and I sank into the comfortable depths of the cushions beside her. 'Have you ordered?'

'No, waiting for you. And I'm dying to hear this news you've got for me.' She jumped up, purse in hand. 'I'll get them — cappuccino for you, I suppose?'

I smiled. 'You haven't forgotten, then!'

'Not after all these years. How could

I?' She chuckled and shook her head, setting her bouncy dark curls bobbing as she set off for the counter.

I watched her short little figure as she crossed the room. We couldn't have been more different in looks, me being two inches taller, with fine blonde hair that went its own way — straight down — regardless of any hairdresser's efforts. They used to call me 'the ice maiden' at school because of my Nordic appearance. And recalling our schooldays brought home to me just how long we had actually known each other. Since we were at the village infants' together in Cornwall where we spent our childhood, that's how long. Over twenty years. Incredible.

Incredible too, that we had ended up living a few miles from each other now, Judy in Beckenham and me here in Croydon, with a convenient tram service between the two.

'Wow — cookies too?' I glanced at the tray as she returned and raised an eyebrow.

Judy shrugged. 'I know I shouldn't, but I've been comfort eating since Hal left. The evenings drag so, you know?'

I patted her hand in silent sympathy. 'I've put on a few pounds though, so I ought to go easy on these.'

She bit into a chocolate chip cookie and looked me up and down. 'You've lost some though, haven't you? Although you always were slimmer than me.'

I nodded and took a sip of coffee. 'It's the stress of that school, Ju. It's what I meant on the phone. I need to talk to you.'

Judy picked up the strain in my voice right away, as I'd known she would. 'Oh dear, whatever's up?' She put down her latte and raised dark eyes to mine. 'Talk away; tell me all about it. Now.'

I gazed down at my cup, stirring the liquid round and round. 'Well, this will come as a shock, but I've given in my notice at the comprehensive. I've resigned.'

'Resigned? Oh. You mean you're

moving to a different school?'

I looked up and caught the expression of 'so what, why all the drama?' on her bewildered face. 'No, it's not like that. You don't understand,' I hurriedly put in. 'I meant I'm giving up teaching. For good.'

'Giving up *teaching?*' Judy's voice rose to a squeak. 'But Jill, *why?* I thought you loved it! It's all you ever wanted to do, right from when we were small. From when you used to line up our dolls and give them 'lessons'.' Her naturally round face turned even rounder with astonishment.

'That was then,' I said flatly. 'As you know, I was off for several weeks last term, suffering from stress, then depression.'

'Yes. But you never really told me what happened.' Her brows met in a frown.

Our drinks cooled on the table as I launched into the whole story. 'It's the discipline problem, Judy. Those kids — well a certain bunch of them — are

4

so stroppy and aggressive. They simply won't sit down and listen, and they make it impossible to teach the ones who are willing to learn. It's not only me — the other staff have the same trouble.'

I glanced at her wide-eyed face. 'And you can't punish them.' I shook my head. 'Even the headmaster has his hands tied. Of course, they know this and exploit it. If you try and keep them in detention after school, you only get the parents storming in and threatening you too.' I sighed and glanced out at the grey and forbidding multi-storey block across the road.

'Ju, I worked my socks off for that school, to the extent that I made myself very ill. The more I did for them, the more work was piled onto me. I used to come in early and stay late. The marking, the assessments, the endless paperwork ... It was taking over my life. But however much I put in, there was no appreciation there, no encouraging word that would have made it all worthwhile.'

I spread my hands, palms up. 'Judy, when I went into teaching, I wanted to make a *difference*. To think I'd achieved something. Helped some kid along the road. But it was impossible. No, Ju, I've had enough. So as I said, I've quit.'

'Oh my! You poor thing. I had no idea it was that tough.' She placed a comforting hand on mine. 'But what . . . have you any idea what you're going to do instead?'

'I've got the germ of an idea that I'll tell you about in a minute.' I raised a hand. 'But first I want to hear your news too.' I picked up my cup again and sat back in the seat. 'I don't suppose you've sold the house yet, have you?'

Judy shook her head. 'No, but it's early days yet; it hasn't been on the market very long. Hal only moved out six weeks ago. Although the divorce was settled long before that, as you know.'

'Yes, I'm really, really sorry about

that. Was it the age difference in the end?'

She nodded and sighed. 'Yes, basically. I can see now with hindsight that what I was looking for when I married him was actually a father figure. But at the time I thought I was in love with him.' She paused. 'And there was a lot more to it than that as well.'

I raised an eyebrow. 'Oh? Want to talk about it?'

'Oh, why not? It's water under the bridge now.' She gazed unseeingly out of the window. 'Hal wanted a family, you see. He loved children and didn't have any by his first marriage. He would have made a wonderful father.'

She turned back to me, her eyes damp. 'But I couldn't. After we both had endless tests, they discovered I couldn't. Having children had never been a big thing to me, but I knew how much it meant to Hal, and I felt terrible about it.' She wiped a hand across her face and rummaged in her bag for a tissue.

7

I squeezed her fingers. 'Jude, I didn't know anything about all this. Why didn't you tell me?'

She sighed and rested her chin on her elbows. 'It all came to a head when you were ill yourself, so I couldn't offload all my troubles onto you when you had so many of your own to cope with.' She shrugged. 'So I let Hal go. Oh, he was sympathetic enough, but I could sense the hurt and disappointment underneath. He took some persuading, but in the end agreed it was for the best. I knew if we went on as we were, his silent reproach would always be there, like the elephant in the corner, you know? The subject that we never talked about, especially whenever we saw a happy family, or a woman with a pram.' She absently stirred her coffee round and round. When she glanced up, she murmured, 'I couldn't live like that, Jill.'

I nodded and she paused, lifting her cup to her mouth, then made a gesture

8

of distaste before pushing it away. 'Ugh, that's stone cold.

'At least the parting was fairly amicable, with no one else involved on either side. That's why Hal was in no hurry to move out. We were living separate lives for a long time. But now he's found a flat not far from his office, so . . . ' She spread her palms and sighed.

'I'm so sorry,' I said, realising how inadequate it sounded. A small silence fell, before I rose to my feet, indicating the cold coffees. 'I'll get some more — same again for you?'

Judy nodded and smiled weakly. 'Minus the cookies, though.'

When I returned, we picked up the conversation where we'd left off. 'So, what are you going to do when the house is eventually sold?' I asked.

Judy's face was solemn. 'I honestly don't know, Jill. I need a change, something completely different. A challenge. I haven't worked for ever so long, because I didn't have to, apart from voluntary stuff; but now I feel a need to do something useful. I shall be comfortably off of course, but I want to earn money of my own instead of living off what came from Hal.'

I understood completely her yearning for independence. But Hal was an executive in an international oil company, and what with the settlement plus half the proceeds of their large house in the prestigious part of Beckenham, 'comfortably off' was an understatement.

We fell silent for a moment, each reflecting on what had been said, before Judy jerked upright, arched her brows and said, 'But what was that 'germ of an idea' you mentioned just now?'

'Ah. Yes.' I bent and reached into my bag for the precious letter.

★   ★   ★

I'd arrived home one day for once with a spring in my step and a sense of well-being that I hadn't felt for weeks. I even found myself humming a little tune as I ran up the steps to the front door, casting an appreciative eye on the colourful tubs of geraniums and petunias on each side.

I remembered how I'd let myself in and bent to pick up the post from the mat. I lived in a little maisonette of my own on the outskirts of the town. It was my haven, my bolt-hole, the first property I'd ever owned, and I felt a momentary pang at the thought of leaving it and starting again somewhere else. But it was full of memories, not all of them pleasant. The moment passed, when I considered what I was escaping from.

I'd glanced at the clutch of letters in my hand. Circulars mostly, pure junk that went unopened, straight into the bin as I entered the kitchen. And one large buff, important-looking envelope. I felt my forehead crease, and with a tinge of apprehension reached for a knife to slit it open. The letter had fallen from my hand as I clutched at the table for support, my legs having turned to rubber and the blood had been pounding in my head as I read it through again.

★   ★   ★

'Have a look at that.' I passed the letter over to Judy and watched her expression change while she read it.

She drew out the several thick pages, prefaced with the usual semi-incomprehensible legal jargon, and skimmed the contents. ' . . . last will and testament of Lorna Harriet Ethel Laity . . . being of sound mind . . . to my great-niece and namesake, Lorna Jill Laity, address unknown, the property known as Creekside Cottage, Penmellin, Falmouth, Cornwall, complete with contents, land and outbuildings . . . with the proviso that she should occupy it for at least part of each year, and keep my beloved garden well-tended.

If not, it is to be sold and the

proceeds donated to the National Trust.'

Witnessed this . . . day . . . '

*   *   *

Great-aunt Lorna! My father's aunt. I only vaguely remembered her. A tall, gaunt figure with blue eyes like gimlets in a tanned and weatherbeaten face, after whom I'd been named, as she said. But I'd dropped the 'Lorna' as soon as I could and opted to use my middle name instead. I hadn't seen her for years. She could have died long ago for all I knew.

'Wow! Aren't you the lucky one?' Judy's face brightened and her brows lifted. 'A cottage in Cornwall, how lovely! You've got a holiday home for life. And you can let it out when you're not there, too, and earn an income from it. Oh, congratulations!' She folded the letter and passed it back to me.

I stowed it away and took a deep breath. I looked down at the tabletop

13

and traced an invisible pattern on it with a fingernail. 'Well now, I've given this a great deal of thought, Ju, mostly when I was laid up at home. So don't think it's a sudden decision at all.' I took a deep breath.

'What I've really wanted to do ever since I recovered is to go somewhere quiet, green and peaceful. And make a really fresh start. So now this bequest has come, it's made up my mind for me.'

'What are you going to do?' She fixed me with a wide-eyed stare.

'I want to go into horticulture. In a commercial way. Growing stuff and selling it. Have a sort of plant nursery.'

'Wh — what? *Horticulture!* You're mad. Stark, staring mad.'

I'd anticipated this reaction and met her astonishment with a level stare. 'Maybe. But you grew up in the country, same as I did, and both our families were connected with the land, right? Especially yours, with the farm — before . . . ' I broke off, not wishing to bring up the sad time when her father had been killed in a tragic accident with some farming machinery.

'You know how my father spends hours on the allotment,' I went on. 'And I think my mum loves her flower garden as much as she loves her family! They both enjoy growing things. So maybe it's in my blood.'

'Ye-e-s. I remember coming to play in your lovely garden. There was a swing under the apple-tree, and . . . '

'That's right.' For a few minutes we wallowed in childhood memories before Judy jerked the conversation back to the present.

'Of course, now I think about it — the way your own house is stuffed with pot plants, and that tiny strip of so-called 'flowerbed' outside the front door, that always looks so lovely, they should have given me a clue.'

'Well, you've got a garden too, although it's mostly trees and grass and I know you don't look after it yourself.'

'True,' she said, nodding. 'Neither

15

did Hal. We employed a gardener.'

'But anyway, Ju — ' I looked her directly in the eye. ' — to get to the point. I was wondering . . . whether you'd like to come into business with me. In a kind of partnership.'

As her jaw dropped I held up a hand and went on before she could interrupt. 'Think about it, seriously. You need something to do. I need a fresh start. We're both at a crossroads in our lives. And Falmouth is an ideal place for growing things — mild and sheltered. They don't call it 'the banana belt' for nothing. And now this legacy. It all fits, don't you think?'

Our eyes met and a silence fell. I could almost hear Judy's mind ticking over. Then at last a broad smile crossed her face and her eyes lit up. 'Do you know, I really think you're on to something,' she said slowly. 'It might even actually work. But I'm going to need a lot of time to think it all over before I make up my mind. My word, what a lot there *is* to think about!'

'I'll say! But now I know you might be interested, I can go into it all a bit deeper. I suggest we both go home now and give it some thought. Then when I've got any news, I'll phone and we can meet up again. How would that be?'

'OK. Fine. Oh, Jill, it's an awesome idea! But I suppose it could be a lot of fun.' Her expressive face lit up with a smile.

'Fun? You *must* be joking — have you any idea of the amount of work entailed in this? If you decide to do it, that is.'

'Of course I have really.' Her voice sobered. 'But seriously, Jill, I'm dying to see the cottage, aren't you?'

'Of course I am. When shall we go?'

'As soon as you like. I can leave the house in the hands of the estate agent, and just go. There's nothing here to stop me.'

I registered the hint of wistfulness in her voice. 'It'll be just what you need,' I replied. 'A change of scene will do you good, and me too.'

* ★ ★

I was thinking back to what Judy had told me of her story. At one time I'd wanted nothing more, either, than to settle down with perhaps a family. But as work took over more and more of my life, I'd thrown myself heart and soul into my career instead — which was now over, and I was feeling bereft.

When I'd been teaching, I had always been under pressure and my social life suffered accordingly. The few men I had been attracted to over time didn't understand what teaching actually entailed; why I couldn't just shut the door on work at the end of the day, like they did.

I jerked myself back to the present. 'So how about next weekend, then?'

'Fine. I'll look up the train times.'

Neither of us had a car, although we could both drive if we had to. Hal had taken his 'gas guzzler' with him when he left, and I had no need of one where I was living at the moment, with its ample public transport.

'And I'll get in touch with the solicitors that sent this letter and find out more details, before we launch off into unknown territory!'

'That sounds as if we're setting off for foreign parts — trekking in the rain forests of Brazil, or exploring darkest Africa!' Another giggle came down the line.

'Get real, woman,' I retorted. 'All this excitement's gone to your head. Look, I'm going now. I'll get back to you as soon as I know anything definite. Bye.'

Seeing Judy and finding that she hadn't dismissed the idea out of hand had cheered me up so much. Now that I could see a way forward, I'd be able to start making tentative plans instead of just daydreaming.

2

I put the phone down and glanced at the clock. Too late to ring Turnbull and Paige today. But I was too unsettled to just do nothing. I wanted to speak to my parents and find out more about Great-aunt Lorna, so I'd call them now.

They still lived in Cornwall, but a long way from Falmouth: right up beyond the expanse of Bodmin Moor, on the other coast, near Launceston, where my younger brother and I had been brought up, and where I'd first met Judy when we'd started school together.

After the preliminary chat with Mum, Dad apparently being out, and the routine exchange of family news, I told her what had happened.

'Lorna? Died, has she?' Her voice rose.

'Yes, didn't you know?' This surprised me, because as far as I knew, we were her only family.

'No. We didn't keep in touch with her, dear. We tried to for years. Your dad went down there sometimes to see her, and took you too, once or twice. But Lorna wasn't interested and not at all friendly. Didn't want nobody, she said. She spoke broad Cornish, worse than me. Anyway, she told your dad she could manage very well on her own. She was quite rude to him, I think. They had a row, I remember, and he more or less washed his hands of her.'

'She sounds a right old harridan.'

'She was always very independent. Not someone you could get close to. Never married, nor had any time for men in her life. Not natural in my view.' I heard a sniff, and could imagine the toss of the head that went with it.

'Well, not everybody does want a man around, Mum.' *And some who do never get to meet the right one*, I could have added.

'Not these days they don't, perhaps, but when she was young it was still a bit unusual. Maybe she had some disappointment in her life, I don't know. Anyway, your dad spoke to one of her neighbours before he came back, as he was still concerned about her, but she said Lorna had become very reclusive and never went out. Always working in her garden, she was. Kept it lovely and grew all her own vegetables and fruit, but never asked anyone inside.' She paused for breath.

'So go on, Mum. What then?'

'Well, it seems like this woman had tried to be friendly too, but Lorna shut the door on her. She was quite put out, and Dad was very upset at the time, I think. So we didn't try and contact her again. She died alone, I suppose — poor old soul. We would have gone to the funeral for all that, if we'd known.'

She paused and took in a sharp breath as if something had just occurred to her. 'Anyway, Jill, how do *you* know she's dead, if we didn't?'

'I had a letter from her solicitors, telling me so.' I hugged my news to myself a little longer, although I was itching to burst out with it.

'You did? B-but, *why?*' There was a note of huffiness in her voice. 'Your dad's her next of kin.'

I took in a deep breath and waited for the explosion that would surely come. 'It's because she's left her cottage to me in her will, Mum.'

'Left her place to *you?* Never! I don't believe it! Are you sure?'

It was exactly as I'd thought. I could almost see her incredulous expression. I suppressed a giggle. 'Of course I'm *sure*, Mother. I just told you. I've had an official letter from her solicitors.'

'But why you?' The implication 'why not us?' hung unspoken in the air. 'You never even knew her, did you?'

'No, but she mentioned that I was her 'namesake'. So I suppose that was why, especially as she'd fallen out with Dad, you said.'

'Oh, of *course* — I'd quite forgotten she was your godmother! That was your dad's doing when we needed an extra woman because you were a girl and had to have two. Before he fell out with her.'

I gasped. This was news. 'And you didn't think to *tell* me?' My voice rose up the scale.

'Well, do you know, it all went out of my head when you were growing up, because I've hardly seen Lorna since. Shortly afterwards she moved down to Falmouth, and you know the rest. Then Mike your brother came along . . . and well, well . . . You'll sell the property, of course.'

'Actually, no, Mum. I'm going to live there.'

'Bring a tidy sum, that will, house prices being what they are, and being so near the river and all . . . *What* did you say?'

'I said I'm moving down there, to live. With a friend. We're thinking of setting up a gardening business with the

24

land that goes with it.'

'*Business?* Whatever for, when you've got a steady job and a career? I thought you were set up for life . . . '

'I've resigned from teaching. You remember how ill I was that time, don't you?'

'Yes, of course I do. But you're all right now. And you mean to tell me you're going to throw it all away because of this *man* . . . ?'

'What man, Mum? There isn't any man.' Mystified, I interrupted her in full flow.

There was an irritated tutting on the other end of the line. 'This friend you're talking about, of course.'

I smiled to myself. 'Oh, it's not a man. It's Judy — Judy Carlyon. You know, Judy from way back.'

'*Judy?* You can't be serious! Are you telling me that you two girls are going to throw up your jobs and your homes and come all the way down here to set up a *business?* In the middle of a national recession? What a pair of fools.

You don't know the first thing about running a business.'

'I know gardening, Mum. And we do have some intelligence. Judy used to work for a building company, remember? She knows a fair bit, and we can learn the rest as we go.'

'Have you any idea what hard work it'll be? Of course you haven't. And well, what your dad'll say I really don't know.'

Needled now, I paused and drew in a breath. 'Mum,' I said firmly, 'you know I love you both dearly, but we are twenty-eight years old, not a couple of dewy-eyed youngsters. And actually, since you mention it, it's not any concern of Dad's.' I stopped short of saying 'nor yours either'. She wouldn't understand, and I didn't want a row and a falling-out.

'Oh, Miss Independence! You're just as bad as Lorna. Not only are you her namesake, you're turning into another like her. Well, don't say you haven't been warned!' And she rang off.

I put the phone down with a heavy heart. I didn't want a family row, but when would she realise I was a fully-fledged adult, capable of making my own decisions and running my own life?

*   *   *

However, by Saturday we were on our way, as excited as a couple of children. I thought back to the ding-dong I'd had with Mum and smiled to myself. If she saw us now she'd be even more sure she had a point.

'So this is it, Ju,' I remarked as the bridge over the river Tamar came in sight. 'Do you get that feeling like I do, of coming home? And of Cornwall being a separate — well, country if you like, as a lot of people think? Somewhere special, anyway to those who were born here?'

'Of course I do. All true Cornish people feel like that. It's where we do belong, my handsome,' she laughed, reverting to dialect. Then, more seriously, she turned and looked me full in the face. 'And Jill,' she said, leaning forward, 'I've decided. Seeing Cornwall again has convinced me it's the right thing to do. So I will come in with you.'

I seized her hand and gripped it. '*Wonderful!* Oh, Judy, I'm so glad! I don't think I could really have done it on my own.' I felt a broad grin spread across my face and, laughing, I raised my bottle of water high. 'Here's to us! And to the future.'

'The future,' Judy echoed, and we toasted it in Adam's Ale.

★　★　★

I sighed with contentment as the train rattled on its way down through the lush green countryside. Small fields edged with thick hedges full of wildflowers flashed past the window, wooded areas with little streams bubbling through them, and at last a glimpse of the sea as we stopped at Par for people changing to the Newquay line.

'Nearly there now,' said Judy some time later, turning from the window to give me a grin.

I nodded. 'Truro next stop.' I began to gather my things together. 'Good thing the train's on time; we'll be OK for our appointment.'

'That worked out really well, with the solicitors being in Truro where we had to change trains anyway.' Judy gave a satisfied nod and hefted her bag onto her shoulder as the train began to slow and the spires of the cathedral came into view.

'Yes — so far, so good,' I replied, making for the door. 'Let's hope it stays that way.'

★   ★   ★

There was a crowd gathered at the end of the aisle waiting to get off and I had to push my way through to retrieve my suitcase from the luggage rack. I'd purposely put it underneath the shelves as it was too heavy to lift up. But now I found it had been moved to make space for the biggest case I'd ever seen, and that someone had placed mine on the topmost shelf of all.

'Oh, look at that!' I exclaimed to Judy without turning round, thinking she was right behind me. 'I can't reach that high! I'll never get it down from there!' I couldn't prevent the wail in my voice, as the crowd around me started to push me sideways in the rush to get out. 'What am I going to do? You'll have to help me.' I turned round to see where she was.

'Let me.' I was brought up short as a tall male figure at my elbow extended a long arm and effortlessly lifted the case down in one hand.

'Oh, thank you! Thank you *so* much.' I looked up at him as I spoke. Then my heart lurched. He was the most attractive man I'd ever seen in my life.

Tall and lean, his soft brown eyes were twinkling with amusement as he must have noticed my jaw drop, and how I was blatantly staring at him.

'No problem,' he drawled, and bent to retrieve his own rucksack. He eased his way through the throng, his lean hips swinging along the platform with an easy stride before I'd even climbed down the steps. Then he vanished into the distance.

★　★　★

Judy and I spent an hour in the offices of Turnbull and Paige, gathering more information about my new property and collecting the keys.

'Your neighbour, Mrs. Pascoe, under our instructions, has been keeping the house aired and clean since Miss Laity's death. When I told her you would be arriving, she offered to get in a few basic groceries too.'

Having dealt with the domestic side of things, we also had the solicitor draw up a legal contract concerning our partnership in the business, should anything go wrong and one of us wanted to pull out.

When all that was signed and sealed, we returned to the station and boarded the next train for Falmouth. Now we were really on our way. A taxi at the other end deposited us at last at Creekside. At Number One, Creekside Cottages, to be precise, as there were three of them in the row.

Three beautiful old stone buildings with roofs of grey slate, they were overhung with swags of honeysuckle and climbing roses. Set in a wooded valley, fields of lush green sloped gently up to some farm buildings just visible at the top. With the view through the trees revealing the sapphire blue of the tidal river beyond, it could have been the perfect rural idyll only seen in dreams.

We both stood unmoving for a moment, overawed, gaping in wonder. Then Judy let out a long breath. 'It is *fantastic!*' she whispered. The silence was so intense we both felt that raised voices would be an intrusion.

'I never dreamed it would be so lovely.' My gaze was riveted on the frontage of my property. 'I have to pinch myself to believe it's real. And that it's actually mine.'

'Well, believe it then, and find the key,' Judy said with a laugh.

Suddenly we were all action, pushing our way in through the overgrown cobbles to the front door. The garden was like a jungle, weeds and plants together, twining and twisting through the bushes that lined the path, and hanging in ropes from the roof of the entrance porch.

For all that, however, the house looked in good condition. The blue front door and windowsills had been freshly painted and the small panes were clean and sparkling.

'Tidden so bad as it do look,' called a sudden voice over the hedge next door, and I jerked around to see a dumpy middle-aged woman poking her head through a gap in the bushes.

'I'm Lizzie Pascoe,' she announced,

withdrawing her head and reappearing at the gate. 'I bin looking after the house since Miss Laity died. Mr. Turnbull employed me, see. 'Tis only the garden what have got out of hand. One of you her niece, are you?' Her little boot-button eyes glanced appraisingly over us.

'Great-niece,' I replied. 'I'm Jill Laity and this is my friend Judy Carlyon.'

'Pleased to meet you. Going to sell the place, are you?' Avid with curiosity in the way of village people, she gazed eagerly from one of us to the other.

'No, we're coming here to live,' I replied.

'*Really? To live?*' Her face lit up in a broad smile. 'So we'll be neighbours then.' She nodded with satisfaction at the news, which would mean that the whole district would know by tomorrow.

'Just the two of you, is it? There's a fair bit of land to look after. What with they two fields up the back, and all this here as well.' She swept a hand around, indicating the state of the garden.

'Yes, there is.' I smiled at her transparency, she was so obviously fishing to see if there was a man on the scene. 'But if my aunt could manage it on her own, I'm sure we can between us.'

'Ess. Thass true.' She nodded. 'Although towards the end of her life she did have a bit of help come in one day a week. Annie Taylor's son Will, that was. Lives at number three, next door to me. He do work at the farm up there — ' She pointed to the cluster of buildings I'd already noticed at the top of the hill. ' — but he'd be willing to give you a hand too, I 'spect, if you do need it anytime.'

'Thank you, er, Lizzie. We'll see how it goes.' I glanced towards Judy, who arched her brows and grinned. 'We're only here for the weekend now, but we'll be moving in permanently as soon as we can.'

The woman nodded and smiled. 'Well, I'll leave you to get on. Anything you want, just let me know.'

Inside, the cottage was just as I'd anticipated, with oak beams, polished wooden floors and small, cosy rooms. I closed the front door behind us and felt instantly at home. The furniture was old but tasteful, some of it verging on the antique. I could certainly live with it and would not need to replace anything immediately. The tranquil atmosphere of the place folded itself around me like a pair of welcoming arms and I knew I would be happy here.

Judy came clattering down the stairs where she'd been inspecting the bedrooms. 'The beds are even made up,' she announced. 'Good old Lizzie. She's certainly done her stuff.'

'Brilliant.' I stifled a yawn. 'Golly, talking of beds, I'm whacked, aren't you?'

She nodded. 'It's been quite a day. But isn't it exciting? I'm going to love it here.'

By the time we'd had a makeshift

meal and taken a preliminary walk around the outside, we were both exhausted and ready for bed. Then I fell asleep to the soothing whisper of the river and the lonely hoot of an owl up in the woods.

*　*　*

Next morning I awoke to the irresistible smells of coffee and toast floating up the stairs. Judy must be up early. I glanced at the clock and gasped. No, it was me who'd slept late. I scrambled into jeans and a cotton top and went down to join her.

'Good morning, lazybones,' she said, grinning. 'You slept well, then.'

'Like a log. Didn't you?' I flopped into a chair at the pine table that was covered with a bright gingham cloth, and rested my elbows on the top.

'I'll say. But the dogs up at the farm were barking earlier and that's what woke me. You obviously didn't hear them.'

I shook my head as she placed a steaming mug in front of me. I took a sip, then picked it up and went to the open door where sunlight was already flooding in. It was going to be another glorious August day.

Absently I registered the clop of horse's hooves coming from the direction of the road that led to the village, over an old 'clapper' bridge. The rider was coming this way; I could see the top of his head bobbing between the trees.

But instead of passing the gate, the horseman stopped when he saw me and reined in his mount. 'Good morning,' he said, raising his crop in greeting.

He was making no move to go on, and it didn't seem very polite to stay where I was, so I wandered down to the gate and leaned over it. As I returned the greeting with my own 'Good morning', he dismounted with one supple movement and came to join me.

Then my stomach turned a somersault. I recognised him. The melting brown eyes were the same. So was the flop of dark wavy hair. And the lithe, lean hips I had last seen swaying down the platform at Truro station were now sheathed in breeches that fitted like a second skin. The long legs were encased in slim leather boots up to the knee, but it was definitely the same man: the stranger who had lifted down my suitcase, and who for some reason had made such a profound impression on me.

3

'I'm Brandon Trelease.' As he extended his free hand I registered long, slim fingers and noticed the ripple of muscle below the blue short-sleeved shirt. He was very tanned, as if much of his time was spent out of doors.

'Jill Laity.' I returned his smile. Then as his hand clasped mine in a firm, warm grip, a bolt of magnetism like lightning shot up my arm and pierced my very core. Shaken, it was a relief to find that Judy had followed me down the path, presumably out of curiosity, and was now standing at my side.

'Ah, so you must be Lorna's niece,' he went on, his eyes meeting mine in a long stare.

'Yes, well, great-niece actually.' I swallowed hard and made an effort to pull myself together. 'And this is my friend Judy Carlyon.' I welcomed the opportunity to break that disconcerting eye contact, as I turned to her. 'Judy, this is Mr. Brandon Trelease.'

'Call me Bran — everyone does.' He shook her hand. 'I farm up there at Tregilly.' He pointed with his crop to the top of the hill. 'My land marches with yours, as I expect you've noticed.'

Judy nodded. 'We took a quick look round last evening. But we're only here for the weekend, so haven't really had time to explore yet.'

'I knew Lorna well.' He glanced towards the house. 'We had our differences, but she wasn't a bad old stick.' He paused and spoke gently to the horse that was rearing up on its hind legs, pawing the air. 'In a minute, Caesar. Calm down.'

As the horse would not be stilled, he re-mounted and wheeled the great animal around, holding it on a tight rein until it settled. Keeping it under control with a touch, he added, 'You'll be putting the property on the market of course, with you living 'up country'.'

The casual remark was at odds with the intense look he threw at me from beneath hooded eyes, and I sensed that my reply to his question mattered rather more than his offhand tone indicated. 'Oh, we're as Cornish as you are.' I smiled. 'Both of us, born and bred. Our roots are here, although the need to earn a living took us away. It's wonderful to be back.'

I glanced away, my gaze travelling over the tranquil rural scene that hadn't changed in centuries, apart from the distant roar of the traffic on the main road to and from Falmouth. This ran beyond the trees edging my property and took a series of sharp bends past the farm above.

'Oh, I see.' He patted the horse's neck. The animal had quietened and was now engrossed in pulling hanks of the sweet grass growing in the verge and noisily chomping it.

Bran raised his head and looked down into my face. 'Only I called to say I'd be the first to offer you a fair price for it.' He cleared his throat. 'No need to go through agents and, er, have all that bother. Um . . . private sale . . . you know . . . to the advantage of both parties . . . '

He was gabbling away now and his voice had assumed an air of urgency. Could he possibly be *nervous?* I wondered, staring up at him. Surely not. But if he wanted to seriously discuss business, why hadn't he dismounted again? Or suggested a meeting in private? Because his height gave him an advantage? Stifling my thoughts, I paid attention to what he was saying.

' . . . I'd be willing to take it off your hands for the asking price . . . '

I raised a hand and interrupted the flow. 'Mr — er, Bran, before you go any further, I must tell you you're jumping the gun here. I've no intention of selling the cottage.' I took a deep breath. 'On the contrary. We're coming here to live.'

'Wh-what? You're going to *live* in it? B-both of you?' His jaw dropped as he looked from one to the other of us in disbelief.

'That's what I said.' I folded my arms and stared him down. 'We'll be moving in just as soon as we can settle our affairs at home and pack up.'

'Oh . . . well . . . I see . . . ' The friendly smile vanished as he jerked the horse's head up and swung the animal round. 'In that case, we shall be seeing a lot more of each other.' His tone of voice made the innocuous remark sound more like a threat than a friendly farewell. 'So I'll say goodbye, just for the time.' He wheeled the horse round a corner and was off in a clatter of hooves down to the bridge again, then up the track towards the farm.

'Wow! He's quite a character.' Judy had been watching the receding chestnut rump and swinging tail, until horse and rider were hidden by the trees. 'The horse isn't bad either.'

'Pedigree. Both of them,' I snapped, not quite knowing why. But something about Bran Trelease's arrogant manner had riled me. 'Used to getting his own way, I imagine.' I turned back towards the house. 'Come on, we've got a lot to do today.'

During the morning we turned out the cupboards and made an inventory of everything that needed replacing. Between us we decided we could supply most things we needed from our own homes. Especially kitchenware.

'These old aluminium pots and pans will have to go,' Judy announced, backing out of a cupboard where she had been rummaging on her hands and knees. 'I'll bring down my nice set of Le Creuset.'

'I've got a food processor that's almost new, and a juicer and, oh, other modern stuff.' I was muttering half to myself as I scribbled away. 'And cutlery. I'll save all of those.' I'd filled one page of the notebook in my hand and turned it over.

'Now to check the bed linen.' I headed for the stairs. 'I don't suppose an old lady would have duvets for a start — she was probably still living in the age of starched sheets and thick woolly blankets!'

That investigation took the whole of the morning, and after a quick salad lunch we headed outside for a thorough look at the exterior of my property. According to the legal agreement we'd had drawn up, Judy would pay me rent for living here, but we would be fifty-fifty partners in the business.

And within the house we would each have our own private space where we could get away from each other if we felt like it. However well we got along, being together all day and every day was bound to become a bit much, and could easily lead to friction.

Fortunately the cottage lent itself to these requirements and would not need any building alterations done. As it was, we could have a bed-sit each and share the bathroom, kitchen and downstairs sitting room.

I was still turning all this over at the back of my mind as we pushed our way through the overgrown garden and took the path leading round to the back of the house.

'The greenhouse looks in pretty good condition,' I remarked, threading my way through a clump of nettles and pushing open the door. 'Ooh, look, a vine.' I pointed to the trailing swags clinging to one side and stretching partway across the roof.

'And it's got loads of grapes coming on it.' Judy glanced up into the green mass. 'We'll be able to have those later.'

'Let's look in the potting shed.' I flourished the key. 'I want to find out what tools are in there and what we shall have to buy new.'

'We shall need more than your aunt ever had if we're going to do this commercially,' Judy remarked, following me inside.

I grunted a reply as I wrote yet another list. 'You bet.' I raised my head and frowned. 'Poly-tunnels for one thing, if we're going large-scale and having a proper nursery business. They can go up in one or other of the fields.'

Then I cast a critical look around the sea of waving weeds and undergrowth. 'Mmm.' I sucked on the pencil in my hand. 'Ju, what do you think of us hiring a rotavator?' I looked closely at her and she raised an eyebrow. 'Just a small one. That would be all we'd need. Because there's no way we can clear this lot by ourselves, and then there are the fields as well.'

'Mmm . . . or we *could* even buy one of our own.' She nibbled her lip as our glances met. 'It would be an investment. Especially if we're seriously going into this business. We could use it over and over, couldn't we?'

I nodded. 'You're right. It would probably work out cheaper than hiring one every time we needed it.'

Judy nibbled her lip, then smiled broadly as our glances met. 'OK, let's go for it! If we're going to be even halfway successful, we've got to have the right tools to do the job.'

'Right, that's settled, then. Now let's

go and look at the fields.'

Two or three stone steps led up the slope to a paling fence with a gate in one corner of it. We leaned our elbows on this and as I glanced over my land, I felt like one of the local gentry surveying his rolling acres.

There were two smallish meadows divided by a stone hedge on top of which a few spindly hawthorn trees bent to the wind. There were brambles everywhere, but covered in blossom, and Judy pointed a finger.

'Look — blackberries to come! Better not chop those bushes down just yet. If we leave them for a few weeks they'll be full of fruit.'

'Our very first crop — and all for nothing!' We chuckled together.

I pushed open the gate and we went inside until we were standing calf-deep in lush emerald-green grass, full of small wildflowers swaying in the breeze. I gripped Judy's arm. 'Look at all this.' I waved an arm. 'We could sell it for hay! That would be a spot of immediate income without any outlay.'

'And we could put the money towards our rotavator.' Her eyes sparkled. 'We're in business already.' Then her face clouded and she frowned. 'Who would we sell it to, though?'

Visions of a haughty mounted figure crossed my mind. 'Who would use hay, Ju? Think about it,' I teased her.

'Well, farmers of course,' she said with scorn. 'But . . . '

'And do we by any chance know any farmers?'

Her eyes widened and she glanced up towards Tregilly. 'Of *course*. You're going to offer it to Bran.'

'Pretty obvious, I'd say.' I gazed at his herd of cows grazing peacefully in a neighbouring field. 'Those animals over there will need feed for the winter. Simple.'

★   ★   ★

By the time we'd finished our tour and cleared some of the most obvious brambles and nettles from around the house, we were tired and filthy. But I was happier than I'd felt for a long time. 'Tomorrow morning before we go back, we'll explore the village,' I said, wiping my dirty boots on the scraper outside the back door.

'Then back home to sort out our stuff,' Judy said with a grin. 'Just think, Jill, the next time we come down it'll be to stay! Isn't it exciting?'

'Awesome,' I replied with a catch in my voice, as the realisation of what we were about to take on forcibly hit me like a punch in the stomach.

★   ★   ★

The village of Penmellin consisted of a couple of streets of originally fine stone-built houses, but these had been altered over time according to the whims of their owners. Decking, balconies and conservatories had sprouted, and some front gardens had been torn up and replaced by block

51

paving or concrete to accommodate the car, or cars.

As well as these now-nondescript houses, there were a few charming old cottages grouped around the parish church, as well as a pub, a Methodist chapel and a general store-cum-post office.

Penmellin, standing at the head of the creek, overlooked a strip of shingle beach where ancient trees sloped down to the water's edge. Their exposed roots clung horizontally to the bank in order to maintain a perilous foothold, where it had been eroded over centuries by the constant ebb and flow of the tides. Small privately owned boats were tied up here, or were cruising about on the incredibly blue water.

Judy waved a hand towards the prestigious-looking headquarters of the local yacht club nearby, and the expensive-looking craft moored in the marina alongside it, and sniffed. 'Plenty of money there, obviously.'

I frowned. 'Incomers, I expect. I can't

imagine local people being able to afford boats like those.'

'Well, when we make our fortune from the nursery, we'll think of getting one for ourselves!'

She was irrepressible, was Judy, and I couldn't help laughing out loud as we descended a flight of stone steps and began to stroll along beside the water.

'Oh, don't those look strange!' I pointed to the pieces of dried wrack and bits of flotsam and jetsam that had been caught up in the leaning branches and hung there waving in the breeze like some kind of grotesque fruit.

'What a heavenly place it is, though,' Judy murmured, stooping to pick up a perfect seashell, delicate pink on the outside with a mother-of-pearl centre. Next to it lay a gnarled, ribbed oyster shell, white as bone, long separated from its other half.

'I read somewhere they dredge for oysters along this coast.' I shaded my eyes and looked out over the creek.

'I wonder if they ever find any pearls,'

she replied dreamily.

There was actually a dreamlike quality about the whole place. I felt if I sat down for a moment I could easily doze off. Maybe it was just a mirage, and when I awoke it would all have vanished, like Brigadoon in the story.

I gave myself a shake. Although considering how hard we'd been working, it was not surprising we were tired. 'Come on, we're leaving for the city again tomorrow. Time we were moving.'

'Wow, what a contrast!' Judy gave a lingering look over her shoulder and followed me.

We wandered slowly back, while over the water the sun was going down in a pool of flame, the sky around it changing as we watched from primrose and apricot to powder-pink, and finally pearly grey as twilight crept in.

Shadows were falling over the village as we climbed the steps from the creek, but even so I recognised the figure in front of us, walking his dog along the quay.

For I'd seen that back view before. I knew that easy stride and narrow hips. Bran.

The dog, on a lead, stopped to sniff at something in the grass verge, and we had no choice but to overtake.

'Well, hello again.' The lazy smile and hooded eyes were mysterious in the half-light, and unsettling. I couldn't put it into words, but there was something about Bran Trelease that I found disturbing, and as my tongue dried in my mouth I couldn't think of a single thing to say to him.

'I thought you would have gone back by now.'

The dog looked up and tugged on the lead, eager to get going again. Tail wagging, he rubbed against me and glad of the diversion, I bent to stroke his head.

'Tomorrow,' Judy replied. 'We're leaving first thing in the morning.'

'Oh, right. Do you like dogs?' Bran

turned towards me and I started. I had been studying the silhouette of his profile, noting the firm jaw, the patrician nose, and the dark hair worn slightly long, curling down over his collar.

'Only Bess tries to make friends with everybody.' He was wearing jeans and a checked shirt open at the neck, with the sleeves rolled back. In the half-light his teeth gleamed very white as he smiled.

'She's lovely.' I recovered my composure and smiled up at him. 'I had a Border collie just like her when I was a child.'

As we were all going in the same direction, Judy and I had no option but to walk with him, so we strolled on a few paces in silence, before Bran slowed and drew in a breath.

'Actually,' he said, gesturing with a hand, 'I'm glad we met. There was something I wanted to ask you. I forgot all about it this morning, and by the time you come down again it'll be too late.'

'Oh?' Wondering what was coming, I glanced up at him as my eyebrows rose.

'Well, it's like this.' He cleared his throat. 'When Lorna was alive, she used to let me mow those two meadows of yours for the hay. I paid her for it, of course. And I was wondering if you'd be willing to let me do that once more? Just this year, I mean, before you start cultivating the ground.'

I almost burst out laughing, and when Judy gave me a dig in the ribs with her elbow, I was glad of the semi-darkness that hid the grin I knew was spreading across my face. 'Well, I suppose so.' I forcibly brought myself under control. 'That all right with you, Judy?'

'Um . . . ' She hesitated, pretending to think it over. 'Ye-es. OK then. If you give us a fair price for it, of course.'

I drew in a quick breath. This was cheeky.

Bran drew himself up to his full height — at least six feet, I thought absently, as he towered over us both.

His tone when he replied was frosty. 'I'll give you the same as I paid Lorna. She was always very satisfied. Right?'

'Yes, of course it is, Bran,' I put in hastily. 'I'm sure that'll be fine.'

We couldn't afford to alienate him. Apart from needing the money, we were going to have to live with him as a neighbour.

'I'll drop the cheque in tomorrow morning early, before you leave.' The voice was still a little cool as we came to the parting of the ways, and with a brief 'Good night' he was gone.

4

The next few weeks were spent in a whirl of hectic activity for both of us, as we cleared out our respective houses and decided what to keep and what to dispose of. I hardly saw Judy, but we spent an enormous amount of time on the phone, deciding who should bring what, so we didn't duplicate. The cottage, although not that small, would only take so much on top of what was already there, which I was keeping.

Eventually I came to the point where my own house was ready to put on the market. I'd been ruthless and had consigned masses of my belongings to the charity shop and the dustbin. For as I was entering a new life, the past could be put firmly behind me, and I didn't need material objects to remind me of it.

That done, I went round to an estate agent and put the house on the market. Not without a stab of trepidation, though. Was I doing the right thing? Stepping out into the unknown with grand plans was one thing; fulfilling them was quite another. But there was always the cottage. If, heaven forbid, our business enterprise did collapse, I could always sell that. After all, I already had a potential buyer, hadn't I? Memories of brooding dark eyes boring into mine, a narrow sensitive face and determined jaw came unbidden into my mind. I shook myself back to the present and swiftly banished them.

★   ★   ★

Judy, having a house three times the size of mine, was bound to take longer over the clearance. However, her ex-husband had taken some of the furniture and all his own belongings when he left, which would make it a little easier for her.

'Oh, Jill!' she wailed down the line one evening, however. 'I'm in such a state. There's still so much stuff here I don't know what to do with, and I'm absolutely shattered.'

I raised my eyes to the ceiling. I was tired too, both mentally and physically. All the planning and wondering, the worry over whether I was really doing the right thing, had all been draining.

'You should take a break. Go out somewhere, have a breather. Shut the door on it all, and when you come back you'll see it differently.'

I tried not to snap; to tell myself Judy had become used to having Hal around to organise things for her. It would be harder for her. I was more used to being independent. It had been a long time since I'd been in a relationship with a man, but this incident brought it all back.

The one I had been closest to had let me down badly. Or maybe he thought I'd let *him* down. A member of staff at the same school, he'd never been able to understand how committed to the job I was.

'Oh, Jill,' he said, spreading his hands in irritation one evening as he called to take me out and found me still marking books. 'For goodness sake — have you forgotten we had a date?'

I jumped up and glanced at the clock. 'Oh, Greg, I'm *sorry*. The time went so quickly . . . and I haven't changed yet . . . or eaten either . . . oh, dear . . . ' I covered my mouth with a hand and stared at him in consternation.

His face had turned brick-red and he was absolutely furious. We'd had a terrible row that evening and he'd walked out, never to return. I wasn't *that* sorry, although I had hoped . . . But he would never understand how I felt compelled to give one hundred per cent to the job I was paid for. I felt I owed it to the students.

But, I sighed, lost in the past, Greg had had more of a *laissez-faire* attitude to teaching. He was quite happy to shut the door and forget it all at the end of the day. I couldn't, and I could never decide even now who had been in the right. Considering it had led me to the brink of a nervous breakdown, but I still wondered.

But that was a long time ago. What had I told Judy? Look forward, not back.

'So, be ruthless like me,' I told her now. 'That's the answer. You're not going to need smart clothes for a start where we're going, and I've seen inside your wardrobe. It's stuffed with high heels, elegant suits and evening dresses. Lovely things, but we shall be living a totally different existence, Ju. If you can't bear to throw them out, you'll have to put them into storage.' A long sigh floated down the line. 'If in doubt, throw it out.' That's my motto.'

'Oh, you're always so organised. It's easy for you to talk.'

I swallowed down my irritation. Judy had always been a hoarder, and with money being no object, I knew how

many kitchen gadgets, china, orna-
ments and knick-knacks she had
accumulated since her marriage. In the
early days Hal had showered her with
expensive presents, and every holiday
abroad had led to more souvenirs and
bric-a-brac.

With a softening of my irritation, my
voice lost its edge. 'Well, if you've got
things you can't bear to part with,' I
said more reasonably, 'maybe you could
store them at your mother's. She's got a
big loft, hasn't she?'

'Oh, Jill, what a brilliant idea!
Whyever didn't I think of that?' Judy's
voice lightened and I could picture the
smile of relief that would be on her
face.

'Because you never think outside the
box? Because you're a ditherer? And a
scatterbrain?' I chuckled softly so she
knew I didn't mean it. 'Seriously
though, Ju, I know this isn't easy
because in the past you always had Hal
to do your thinking for you. But it'll do
you good to get your independence

back and learn to stand on your own two feet again. Be like me — put the past firmly behind you and look forward, not back.'

'Yes, you're absolutely right. It will, and I shall.' A note of determination had crept into her voice.

I drew in a breath and let it out in a long sigh, realising where my duty as a friend lay. If we were going to be free to return to Cornwall in the not-too-distant future, I would have to offer, or we'd be stuck here forever.

'I'll come round and give you a hand, if you like. I'm almost through here.' I tried to sound light-hearted, although I'd really rather not. I'd seen enough of plastic bags, packing cases and cardboard boxes for the time, and was just not in the mood; but on the other hand I did genuinely feel sorry for her.

'Oh, Jill, that would be *wonderful!* Thank you so much,' came the enthusiastic reply. I shrugged my shoulders, resigned to it, and knew I'd done the right thing.

★   ★   ★

A few weeks later we were on our way, this time for good. As excited as a couple of schoolgirls, we arrived in a taxi loaded down with bags and cases. Having brought all we would need for now, we had arranged a carrier for the rest, which would be delivered in the next day or two.

'Oh, look — the hay's been cut.' Judy craned her neck to see over the fence as we dragged our stuff up the path.

'Wow, doesn't it make the fields look different?' I paused with the door key in my hand as I followed her pointing finger. 'Bigger. And I suggest we put the money from that cheque of Bran's towards the rotavator, like we said. What do you think?'

'Yes, that's fine by me. Then we can start turning over the ground. Let's trawl the internet tonight and search. We might even find a second-hand one in good condition.'

'Mm,' I grunted, bent double as we

dragged all our luggage inside and piled it in the living room to be sorted later. 'We could order the poly-tunnels at the same time.'

Judy nodded. 'We'll need to get those fixed up before the winter. Then we can work in them whatever the weather.'

'And we can start on the garden while we wait for them to come. Gosh, what a lot there is to be done!'

'So the sooner we begin — ' My mouth widened in a huge yawn, and I flopped onto the sofa with a sigh. ' — the better.'

And as Judy did the same, we both burst out laughing.

★　★　★

We spent the next couple of days settling in, stocking up on food and generally sorting ourselves out.

'Another big item we're going to need,' I said as we panted up the steep hill from the village shop, loaded with groceries, 'is a vehicle of some sort. We

67

shall have to have transport anyway, when the business gets going, and even now just to get to a supermarket, or into Falmouth. That shop is handy for small things, but expensive, didn't you think?'

'Mm.' Judy stopped to change hands with her carrier bags. 'Absolutely. I know we passed a garage and car sales place when we were in the taxi.' She wrinkled her nose, thinking. 'But I can't remember now how far it was.'

'Lizzie'll know. We can ask her.'

'Ask her what?' We both jumped, startled, as Lizzie Pascoe bobbed up from behind her garden wall, where she'd obviously been pulling up weeds. A broad smile across her round face, she wiped her hands in her apron and passed one elbow across her forehead.

'Phew, some warm still, idden it?' She drew in a breath. 'I knew you was back — saw the lights on other evening. Here to stay now, are you?'

'Hello, Lizzie. Yes, we are. We were saying that we ought to buy a car now we're settled here, and that you would probably know the name of that garage down the road. They had used cars for sale there.'

'Oh, Rodda's place, you mean. Yes, he's all right, is Arthur. Won't do you down nor nothing. You can trust Art. Know anything about cars, do you?'

I shrugged. 'Not much, but . . . '

'Tell you what, then. I'll get Will Taylor to come down there with you, shall I? Born on wheels, he was; nothing he don't know about engines. He can give you a lift — 'tis a fair way to walk.'

'Oh, yes please Lizzie.' Judy and I glanced at each other and spoke in unison, then laughed. 'That would be wonderful.'

Her face creased in a broad smile of satisfaction. I guessed there was nothing Lizzie liked better than to be involved in other people's business. But she was a good-hearted soul, busybody or not and, I thought shrewdly, we were going to rely on her local knowledge in all sorts of ways like this.

'Thass all right, then. I'll tell Will when he do come in for his tea. Ploughing over to Tregilly they are, up the top field over the road, he and mister.'

I now became aware of the drone of the tractor in the distance, a sound that I'd been hearing all day in my subconscious mind, but hadn't registered.

'Thanks a lot, Lizzie.' We picked up our baggage and turned for the gate.

'You're welcome, my handsome. Anything you want to know, just ask. I'll see you later on.' Her head went down behind the wall again as she bent to resume her weeding.

'A good thing we weren't saying anything bad about her,' I murmured when we were out of hearing.

'That's village life for you,' Judy said with a rueful smile. 'You have to learn to hold your tongue when you're out. Remember when we were children? We never dared to get up to much mischief, knowing the lace curtains would be twitching and tales would get back to Mum before we did!'

* * *

We slept solidly that night, and I was woken up by the slanting autumn sunlight sending golden bars across my bed. I hadn't drawn the curtains as my room wasn't overlooked. I'd been lulled to sleep by a soft breeze rattling the dry leaves in the nearby woods and the cooing of a late-roosting pigeon.

I threw back the covers and made for the bathroom. This weather was too good to waste a minute. Then, as soon as we were up and breakfasted, we headed for the garden.

'While the weather's so glorious, we must get as much clearance done as possible,' I remarked, pulling on tough boots and tucking my oldest jeans into them.

It was warm enough to work without a sweater, so I'd turned out an old faded red shirt of brushed cotton I'd had for years. It was ironic that I'd sent most of my good clothes to the charity shop, and kept my well-worn ones, instead of the other way round. I'd piled my hair into an untidy knot on top of my head, knowing it would eventually unravel as it always did, but at least it was out of my eyes for a while.

Judy appeared wearing cord trousers and a blue T-shirt, lacing up her boots as she came, her bouncy curls looped up in a ponytail, hazel eyes twinkling.

'Right, we look the part. Now to get down to it. Come on.' I grinned as I led the way outside and we paused to look around.

We were now into early September. Fat bees were lazily working the heavy-headed dahlias of gold, pink and white, while others were buzzing about the tall Michaelmas daisies of regal purple that waved in the beds nearest the path.

I raised my face to the sun and gave a sigh of content. I'd never really appreciated weather when I lived in London. Never looked up at the sky much at all, being too busy rushing about and thinking of the next task waiting to be done. Rain had just been a miserable nuisance, whereas here I imagined, it would be an integral and welcome part of the cycle of growing things.

There were four large flowerbeds in all, shaped like pieces of pie, forming a circle around a paved area. This was sheltered from the wind by a tall privet hedge badly in need of trimming back, like everything else, between the garden and the road. Obviously someone had had the foresight to plant that as a windbreak many years ago.

In the centre of the circle was an ancient sundial. Picking my way through the weeds, I rubbed at the green moss and encrusted dirt with my shirt cuff to read out the inscription.

'Though seasons come and go,
    and years fleet by,

Love cannot change or friendship
   die.'

'Oh, isn't that *lovely?*' Judy sighed,
looking over my shoulder. 'But I never
know how to tell the time by one of
these, do you?'
'I think you just have to look at the
shadow, and which number it's pointing
to.' I glanced up and smiled. 'But I
don't suppose you can alter it for
British summertime!'
I turned back to the main path.
'Come on. We *must* start work or the
morning will just slip by.'
I looked carefully around. The beds
were stuffed full of hardy perennials,
small shrubs and some annuals that had
self-seeded and sprung up haphazardly
wherever the fancy took them.
'Judy, if we saved the seeds from
those,' I said, pointing, 'we'd have the
basis of some stock for next year. Look,
there's some love-in-a-mist over here,
opium poppies at the back . . . '
   ' . . . and under these shrubs here I

can see forget-me-not seedlings, and night-scented stock. Oh, and wallflowers that have sprouted from last year, too.'

'Oh, brilliant. Now, let's save what we can from those and then start pulling up and cutting back what's left.'

'OK. I'll go and get the wheelbarrow for the rubbish and see if I can find containers of some sort for the seeds.'

'And labels so we don't mix them up.'

We worked steadily all morning in different areas, and I had to stand up to stretch my aching back every so often, unused as it was to such hard labour. But it was exhilarating too. Here the pace of life was so much slower and quieter. I could see placid cows standing in the shade of a group of sycamores up in the field, and hear small birds chirping from the overgrown shrubs above my head.

Yes, I decided, being close to nature was very soothing, and put things in perspective. Nothing here could be more different from the hectic life I'd just left. The new term would be just beginning now. I smiled to myself as I thought if any of the parents or staff of the school could see me now — the former so-smart Miss Laity — they wouldn't recognise this grubby, scruffy woman bending her back once more to scrabble about on her hands and knees in the soil.

★ ★ ★

By lunchtime we had accumulated a vast pile of weeds and clippings.

'What are we going to do with this lot? And the stuff that's still to come?' Judy put the barrow down and wiped a hand across her grimy face. I realised I must be looking the same, plus my hair had come down as I knew it would, sticking in tendrils to my hot forehead and probably looking like a bird's nest. But what if it was? We weren't going anywhere or seeing anybody. Bliss.

We had wheeled all the rubbish, load

by load, through the gate at the end of the garden and into the bottom field. Now we were leaning on the paling fence, drawing breath and cooling off.

'I don't really know. It'll have to stay where it is for now, under the hedge. Unless — ' I glanced towards her as a thought occurred to me. ' — I wonder if we'd be allowed to light a bonfire? Some places have restrictions, don't they? Because of air pollution or something.'

'Don't know.' Judy slowly shook her head and shrugged. 'That's something else we can ask Lizzie.'

'Or me,' came a voice, and I whirled round to see Bran's tall figure striding towards us.

5

He emerged from the bend in the track that led down from his property and past ours. Up until now he had been screened by the hawthorn hedge that ran alongside it, which was why we hadn't seen him coming.

'Oh, Bran! Hello.' My hand had flown involuntarily to my tangled hair and I was very conscious of the dirty state I was in. Well, we both were; we'd been grubbing in the soil for hours. And anyway, why should it matter?

In contrast, Bran was clad in a spotless cream-and-green short-sleeved top over cropped cargo pants of grey cotton. His bare arms were very tanned, as was his face. Behind him trailed Bess the collie, wagging her plumy tail as she came up to us. As she poked her nose under the fence I bent to stroke her soft coat, glad of something to do with my hands.

'What were you going to ask Lizzie about?' He looked quizzically at me, arching one dark brow. 'Can I help at all?'

Judy replied as I stood there for a moment lost for words, somehow finding it difficult to pull away from that intense gaze.

'We were wondering whether we're allowed to light a bonfire to get rid of all our rubbish, or if there's a ban on them around here. That was all.'

'Oh, that's easily answered,' Bran said, switching his attention to her.

I took a deep breath and straightened up, feeling a weakness in my legs that I hadn't been aware of before now. I put it down to the kneeling and bending I'd been doing all morning. After all, I wasn't yet acclimatised to such hard physical work.

'Yes, it's perfectly all right to light a fire,' Bran was saying. 'I sometimes have one myself. We're far enough out in the country not to be a nuisance to other people.' He brushed a wavy lock of hair, dislodged by the breeze, back from his forehead.

'Oh, good.' I recovered myself. 'We can have it here in the field before we turn the soil over.'

'Are you going to get someone in to do that?' Bran took a long look around him. 'You won't be able to manage all this by yourselves, of course.'

His condescending tone irritated me and I tilted my chin to look him in the face. 'We shall, actually,' I retorted. 'We're going to get a rotavator to work on it.'

Both eyebrows shot up this time, and he gave a low whistle. 'Really?' he drawled. 'Have you ever used one before?'

'No, but we can learn. Two small fields shouldn't be a problem.' I stared him down until he had to look away.

'It'll be harder than it looks.' Bran swept a hand around, his gaze following the lie of the land. 'For one thing, it's on a slope; and for another, it hasn't ever been tilled to my knowledge. Lorna used to let the fields out for grazing in the winter when she was alive.'

'Oh, we like a challenge,' I replied briskly, 'don't we, Judy?' She followed my lead and nodded, but I could see her heart wasn't really in it.

Bran turned away and whistled up the dog, who was on the far side of the field sniffing for rabbits in the hedge.

'Well, if you find it's too much for you when you come down to it,' he remarked in a casual tone, 'let me know. I'll send someone over to give you a hand.'

'Thank you.' I bit off the tart reply that was on the tip of my tongue, until he'd proceeded on his way and had reached the road at the bottom — which ran past the front of our house. So we would probably see a lot more of him if he used that track very often. As presumably he would, for the only other way was by the busy main road beyond the hedge, dangerous on foot at any time as it had no pavement.

'Patronising prig!' I burst out, and Judy turned to me with a puzzled expression.

'Patronising? Why? He was only offering to help. I thought it was kind of him. He seems a nice person.'

'Huh.' I glowered at her. 'Insinuating that we're hopeless females who can't manage without help from a man, more like.'

'Jill, whatever's come over you?' Her eyes widened. 'One day we might be very glad to accept his offer.'

'Not in a million years,' I growled. 'Now come on, we need to get cleaned up. Plus, it's lunchtime and I'm famished.'

*   *   *

We spent the rest of the day in a similar fashion, by which time we seemed to be actually making a difference. One whole patch of the garden was weed-free and we had saved several cartons of seeds for planting in the spring.

Healthily tired, in the evening we gathered round the computer to research the equipment we needed. After several dead ends, we eventually struck gold on eBay, where a retiring gardener was selling off his power tools before going to live abroad. A short phone call and a chat with him confirmed that his type of machine was exactly right for our purposes, and he had a few other things we could do with as well, all at a reasonable price as he wanted a quick sale.

The short call turned into one lasting over an hour, as he sounded so interested in our project we couldn't get away. But after a lifetime of gardening, both for himself and for other people, the old man was full of advice that he thought would be useful.

'Wey hey!' I put the phone down and did a 'thumbs up' to Judy, who had been leaning on my shoulder listening to the conversation. 'How about that? Lucky or what?'

'Yeah, I should say so!' And, tiredness forgotten, we hugged each other and did a little twirl of sheer delight.

*   *   *

I'd never slept so well or so deeply as I was doing at Creekside. The combination of fresh air and hard physical work had us both eating like horses and falling exhausted into bed each night.

We were gradually acquiring a late-summer tan as well, and my hands, even with wearing gloves, were blistered and scratched. They bore little resemblance now to the manicured perfection I was once so proud of. And my teaching career, which once had filled my world, now seemed so remote and long ago, it could have been in some former life.

Then came the great day when our equipment arrived. As an enormous carrier's van drew up outside the house, I could sense Lizzie's antennae swing into action next door, and knew she'd be round as soon as it had gone.

We were poring over the rotavator and studying the handbook that had come with it, when her head appeared over the hedge. 'Dear life!' she exclaimed. 'Some great thing, idden it? You going to ask Will Taylor to work it, are you? Like I said, he'd be willing to give you a hand. Heavy going, that'll be.'

Not again! Controlling my impatience with difficulty, I managed not to snap at her. 'Lizzie, it's not much bigger than a lawn mower. We can manage perfectly well, thank you.'

'Oh, well,' she bridled, lifting a shoulder, 'only trying to help, that's all.'

I hastened to pacify her. We couldn't afford to fall out, living as close as we did.

'Yes, I know.' I gave her a beaming smile. 'And we do appreciate it, really. I expect we *shall* need to get Will in one day for other heavy stuff.'

I changed the subject. 'And you did say he'd give us a lift down to the garage, didn't you? That would be really good. Would you ask him when you see him next?'

'Of course I will. I'll catch him when he do come in for his dinner, and remind him. He'll call round, shouldn't wonder.' All smiles now that she was properly involved, she moved away. 'Well, I must get on. Things to do. Can't stand here chatting all day. See you later.'

* * *

Partway through that evening a knock came at the door, and I opened it to find a burly figure with a mop of tousled fair hair standing on the step. I guessed who he was before he held out a hand and smiled broadly.

'Hi, I'm Will Taylor.' Thirty or so I guessed, with the bluest eyes I'd ever seen on a man. I grasped the huge hand, brown and calloused from physical work in the open air, and smiled back.

'Jill Laity.' I stood to one side of the low doorway. 'Do come in.' He bent his head with accustomed ease to avoid the granite lintel as a matter of course, as all three cottages were built alike. 'This is my friend and business partner, Judy Carlyon.'

Judy turned from the sink where she'd been washing up, and wiped her hands on the tea towel. 'Hello, have a seat. Would you like some coffee, or a cup of tea?'

'No, thanks very much. Just had one.' He looked appraisingly round the room and sat down on the oak settle with his back to the window. 'How are you shaking down, then? Like it here, do you?'

'Oh, yes!' we said together and laughed.

He leaned forward, elbows on his knees. 'I used to come here a fair bit when your auntie was alive — did some jobs for her off and on. Haven't changed the place much, have you? You're keeping her furniture and stuff, then?'

'Oh, yes, we think it's fine as it is. Full of character, you know?'

He nodded and straightened up. 'Well now, Lizzie was saying you do want a car, and you're going down Arthur's to see about one. I can take you over there tomorrow morning if you like. Got to go into Falmouth, so I can drop you on the way and pick you up on the way back. That be all right?'

'That would be wonderful, thanks a lot.'

'I know a bit about engines meself. Worked in a garage once. I dearly love tinkering around with motor bikes and such. Used to drive Mother mad with coming in covered with grease and oil, I did. She was thankful when I went up the farm to work instead.' He chuckled and rose to his feet. 'Anyway, I won't keep you. Ten o'clock all right for you tomorrow, is it?'

'Lovely. Thanks, Will; and if you could have a look over the engine of this car on the way back — supposing we get one — we'd be really grateful.

Not that I wouldn't trust Arthur,' I hastily added, 'but . . . '

Will grinned. 'A second opinion would be even better.'

I smiled back and nodded.

'OK then, I'll see you tomorrow. Bye.'

'He seems nice.' Judy stood looking out after she'd seen him to the door and gave an answering wave, as Will raised his hand and closed the gate behind him. 'What a huge man. Did you see the width of those shoulders?' She closed the door and went back to finish the dishes.

'Mm.' I was thinking how fortunate we were with our neighbours. Living as close as we did to the other two cottages, and to the farm, could have been so much different. As it was, we had support from all sides if we needed it. Although, on the other hand, our every move seemed to be monitored, and could easily sap our independence if we let it.

I jumped as another knock came at

the front door, and went to answer it, expecting Will to have come back. And was brought up sharp as Bran's tall figure loomed out of the twilight shadows.

'Oh, Bran!' My heart began to thump. 'It's you! I thought . . . I wasn't . . . er . . . ' Stupidly flustered, I stepped back and widened the doorway. 'Do come in.'

'Thank you.' He bent his head and stepped inside.

'Come through.' I indicated the sitting room.

'Ah, no, I don't think so.' He glanced down at his feet and shuffled them on the mat. 'I'm too muddy. This will do.'

He glanced around the kitchen and nodded to Judy. 'I hope I'm not intruding . . . um . . . on your mealtime or anything?'

'No, not at all,' she replied and repeated her offer of tea or coffee.

'No thanks, I won't.' He sat down in Will's vacated place with his back to the window. 'I've just come to discuss . . .

er . . . a bit of business with you.'

'Oh? What sort of business?' I sat down opposite him in the rocking chair next to the Rayburn, and Judy perched on the little footstool beside me. Bran was looking steadily at me as he spoke, and I realised that in the failing light, he could see my face and my reactions much better than I could see his.

'Well, it's like this.' He leaned forward. 'You recall I once offered to buy this cottage, and you refused to consider it?'

'Of course I do. And as you can see — ' I extended a hand and glanced around the room. ' — we're well and truly settled here now, and have even less intention of moving.'

Bran nodded. 'Of course. I didn't think any other. But I have another proposal to put to you.' He cleared his throat, leaned back and stretched out long legs in blue jeans in front of him. He was wearing a navy Guernsey over an open-necked checked shirt. The V-shape of his neckline was very tanned and a few dark hairs nestled in the crease . . . I jerked my attention back to what he was saying.

'It's like this. I suppose you've seen those barns at the top of the field, just across the yard from our back door.'

'Yes, of course.'

He'd said 'our' back door. My attention drifting again, I wondered who 'we' were. Was he married? In a relationship? With a family? I'd never noticed anyone else coming and going up there, or heard children's voices. But then, I hadn't really thought about it. I didn't know why I was speculating like this now. It was pointless, and absolutely none of my business.

'Well, they're unused now, just standing idle, and I have plans to turn them into holiday homes. You've seen barn conversions on other farms, I'm sure.' Bran arched an eyebrow.

'Oh, yes,' Judy replied. 'My parents did the same once on the farm where I used to live.'

'Really?' He turned to her with a

smile. 'Well, you'll understand the problems that come up when you try to do these things.' He paused. 'Getting planning permission for an access road is my own particular problem.' He sighed. 'The front of the farm, of course, has a drive leading out onto the main Falmouth road. That was built long ago. But since then the road's been widened, and has become three times as busy since all those new houses went up in that development above the village.' He sighed again and spread his hands wide. 'So they turned down my application, because the drive now opens just a few yards from that double roundabout they put in.'

I nodded, wondering what on earth all this had to do with us. Vaguely I was aware as Judy crossed the room and switched on the light, with some remark about the evenings drawing in . . . soon be time to put the hour back . . .

'So,' Bran finished, and now as the room flooded with light, I could see the bleak expression on his face. 'The conversion's not going to happen unless I can find alternative access. Somehow.'

'Oh, yes. I see.' I kept my tone polite and non-committal, as a hint of what might be coming crossed my mind.

'Which is why I'm here tonight.' He swivelled his full attention to me. 'Because, Jill, I'm wondering now whether you would consider selling a strip of your land that runs parallel to the lane.' He paused, presumably to let this sink in.

I felt my eyes widen, but suppressed my indignation and the sharp retort that was on the tip of my tongue.

'Then that track could be widened into a road, and would exit on the quieter route outside here.' He gestured over one shoulder with a pointing thumb. 'It's the only way I can possibly see around the problem.' He glanced expectantly at me.

I drew in a sharp breath as, seeing red, I jumped to my feet and rounded on him. 'You *must* be joking!' My voice rose up the scale with rage. 'Do you really think I'd carve up my land and leave us exposed to a public *road?* Purely for *your* convenience? What a preposterous idea!' My head was whirling. I couldn't get over the sheer arrogance of it. 'You honestly expect I'd let you ruin the peace of this idyllic place with the noise of traffic, people, children, dogs . . . going up and down almost outside our window, just for *your* benefit?' Hands on hips, fully aware I was yelling like a fishwife but unable to stop, I glowered at him.

'Jill, this is so important to me.' His jaw was set, his eyes flint-hard as he rose to his feet and gazed fiercely back at me. 'You've no idea how important,' he added under his breath, turning restlessly on a heel. 'So much so that I'm willing to make it worth your while.' He faced me again and paused. 'Of course I don't want to jeopardise your privacy — there will be a high dividing wall, I promise.'

His calm and measured tone was

such a contrast to my own show of temper that I almost felt ashamed for yelling so.

'And,' he went on in the same even tone, 'I'm prepared to offer you a very good price.'

The sum he named brought me up short and I drew in a swift breath. It *was* a generous offer, as he'd said. And we'd had so much outlay since we came here. We'd bought all our equipment, including the rotavator, and now a car. Soon there would be bills coming in — for road tax and insurance, for electricity, water, the phone, plus fuel for the Rayburn over the winter months, and the running costs of a vehicle. Neither of our houses was sold yet, which I'd been relying on; and apart from selling the hay, to date we hadn't earned a penny from our infant business. Nor would we until the spring. I swallowed hard as the implications of what we'd taken upon ourselves loomed large, and swiftly silenced the echo of my mother's voice whispering in my ear: 'You know *nothing* about business . . . '

And the hole in my savings was growing bigger by the day. However, pride forbade me to ask Judy to input any more of her money. I knew she would of course, without question, but our arrangement had been strictly fifty-fifty in everything.

And of course I'd no intention of accepting Bran's offer. So I gritted my teeth, tilted my chin and met his direct gaze. At the stark pain I saw in his eyes I almost relented and reconsidered his offer. But only almost. I drew in a breath and quickly broke the eye contact.

'No, I think not. Our privacy is priceless, and worth more than any money.' I shook my head as I pointedly opened the door.

Bran left without another word.

6

'Phew, Jill, you flew off the handle a bit there, didn't you?' Judy closed the door behind Bran and turned to me wide-eyed. 'That was a lot of money he offered. And you didn't even consider it.'

Oh, not you too, I thought and gritted my teeth. For we mustn't fall out, ever. It would be a death-knell to all my hopes and dreams.

'You don't mean — you thought I was wrong, do you?' I glared at her as she came back into the room.

Leaning on the back of a chair, she gazed at me. 'Well, I thought you were being a bit hasty.' Biting her lip, she looked away. 'And I did think, too, that you could have consulted with me before you decided so abruptly. I know it's your property, but we *are* partners in this. Or at least you could have told

Bran you'd think about it.'

Contrite, I reached for her hand and squeezed it. 'Oh, Ju, I'm so *sorry*. You're absolutely right, of course. It's just that I saw red and reacted instantly. You know how quick-tempered I am.'

Judy smiled. 'Oh yes, I should be used to that by now. Act first and think afterwards, that's the story of your life!' I laughed, but she was right. I took in a breath and let it out on a long sigh.

'It was that arrogance of his again — assuming that if he waved enough cash under my nose we'd be willing to dance to his tune.'

'Well, I didn't see it that way at all,' Judy said reflectively. 'I saw Bran's face when he was on the way out, and you didn't. The way his shoulders slumped. He looked defeated, Jill — and shattered, as if this was the last straw. Not a bit arrogant. He seemed almost — um — how shall I put it? Vulnerable, that's the word. As if his world had fallen apart.'

'Pooh! Pure imagination.' Meeting

her eyes I pointed a finger. 'And we both know you've always had a lively one!'

Judy shrugged. 'OK, tit for tat,' she said, resigned, and would have looked away if I hadn't rounded on her.

'So, what do *you* think about having our privacy shattered by a public road running past this house? Is that what you want?'

She sighed and moved restlessly around the room. 'No, of course not. I only wish we could come to some kind of compromise, that's all. For Bran's sake.'

'For *Bran's* sake?' I felt my brows rise. 'Judy, whose side are you on in this?' I glared at her and she reddened. 'Anyone would think you fancied him.'

'Don't be ridiculous,' she snapped. 'I hardly know the man.' She turned her back and began clattering dishes, putting them away in the dresser cupboard as if her life depended on it.

I frowned as I gazed thoughtfully after her, and wondered. Wondered, too, at the strange sensation that flared up inside me and was gone in an instant.

* * *

By lunchtime next day we were the proud possessors of a small white builder's-type van, roomy enough to use for transporting or delivering plants, convenient for shopping trips and not too big to park in the lay-by outside the cottage. Our differences forgotten, we decided to try it out with a shopping trip into Falmouth that afternoon.

'Shall I drive one way and you the other? We're both bound to be a bit rusty after all this time.'

Judy nodded as I took the wheel. 'Fine by me. That way we can both get back into practice. I don't suppose it will take us very long.'

It didn't. I soon felt the old skills coming back. The van was easy to drive and purred through the traffic-free country lanes with no trouble. By the time we came to the busier main road I was fully confident, and when we reached the town I reversed into a parking space with a minimum amount of effort.

We'd parked on Custom House Quay, looking over the deepest natural harbour in western Europe. There was no wind and the calm water was a sheet of silvery steel, the gulls like scraps of paper drifting above it on the air currents. Several large ships flying foreign flags lay at anchor, probably waiting to pull into the docks for repair, and smaller boats of all kinds skimmed about on their own concerns.

Across the bay the colours of the land behind St.Mawes were muted in the late-autumn light. Pastel shades of plum, ochre, and chestnut-brown lay over the fields and distant trees. Nature was gradually slowing down, preparing for the winter ahead.

'Oh, doesn't it feel good to take time off from work for once?' Judy remarked with a smile, as we left the car park and turned up the incline towards the town.

'Mm.' I nodded. 'It does feel a bit like a holiday. It must be because of the sea. But it won't last long, so let's get shopping.'

'Oh, look, there's the King's Pipe. Remember that?' I pointed to a tall chimney beside the path.

Judy nodded. 'Where they burned all the contraband tobacco brought in from overseas. I remember coming down here on a school trip once and being told to read that plaque. We had to write an essay about it afterwards, for homework.'

We spent a pleasant afternoon pottering about the town, as much for pleasure as for getting what we needed. After a leisurely cup of tea in a café overlooking the water, we were forced to leave at last, as the waiting time in the car park had almost run out.

'We can always come again,' I remarked as we loaded parcels into the back. 'But right now, it's back to the grind!'

* * *

As winter drew in and we could do less and less outdoor work, I spent a lot of my time studying gardening catalogues and planning for spring.

I was curled up in the basket chair beside the Rayburn one evening, going through the latest batch. We more or less lived in the kitchen, drawn there by the cosiness of the range. It seemed a waste to heat the other room when we had that.

'There's a good offer on plug plants in this one.' I waved the booklet at Judy, who was sitting at the computer sending e-mails to her friends.

'What kind of plants?' She swivelled round in the chair and shifted her attention to me.

'Oh, all sorts. Pansies, pinks, fuchsias . . . too many to tell. You'll have to look through it yourself.' Judy reached out a hand and after passing the catalogue over, I drew up my knees and clasped my hands round them, deep in thought.

'If we bought in a load of those,' I said at last, 'we could bring them on in the greenhouse and they'd be ready to plant out in the spring. And it's not too early to sow sweet peas, either.' I was thinking aloud and talking almost to myself. 'That way we could have everything ready just when people start thinking about their gardens again. It would be a good way to kick-start our nursery — those are all popular plants and I'm sure they'd sell.' My brain was doing overtime as I saw more and more opportunities opening for our infant business. 'Then next year we can sow seeds of our own, and sell our own plugs too, instead of buying.'

'Mm.' Judy was turning the pages, engrossed. 'And bulbs, Jill,' she said, raising her head. 'We must plant loads of bulbs in containers. Soon, because they'll be just ready for the Christmas market. They make good, inexpensive presents.'

'Good thinking. There are loads of flowerpots and other containers in the shed that we can use. At least that's one thing we shan't have to buy.' I straightened up and went across to the table. 'Let's make a list and send off the order right away.'

Judy closed down the computer and came to join me. 'And I thought there wouldn't be much to do in the winter months!' she laughed.

'We've got to think about advertising, too,' I remarked as we flipped over pages together and marked possible purchases of stock. 'It's no good having plants to sell if nobody knows we're here.'

'That's right. In the local paper, and yellow pages, and posters in shop windows . . . '

Judy was chewing the top of her pen and staring into space. 'We ought to have a sign to hang outside here, too. Jill, what are we going to call our business?' she asked, frowning. 'It has to have a name before we can advertise at all. Something that people will remember.'

'Well, actually I was thinking the same thing in bed last night.' I turned towards her as our glances met. 'And I was wondering, what do you think about calling it the 'Two Jays Nursery'? After our initials, I mean.'

'Jill, I love it!' Her face lit up with enthusiasm. 'That's a brilliant idea. I'm sure there's not another place called that anywhere. And hey!' She gave me a dig in the ribs. 'We could have a sign painted with two jays on it — you know, the *birds!*'

'Oh, *yes!* Well done. What a great team we do make! And jays are really colourful; they'd look lovely on a signboard. I can see it already, can't you?'

As we scrubbed flowerpots, cleaned out the greenhouse and washed the windows, brushed all the ancient debris out of the potting shed and other mundane tasks, I kept thinking of what Jill had said about my reaction to Bran's offer. And the more I thought about it, the more I realised how rude I must have sounded. I really ought to apologise to him, but it was too trivial a matter to make a special visit up to the farm. I didn't know what to do.

The small problem lay niggling at the back of my mind all the time I was working, a constant irritating distraction. Then one day along came the perfect opportunity. It was a calm, mild day for November. Under a sky of pearly grey, the dark silhouettes of a stand of trees on the skyline stood out like a frieze of black lace; and the air, although chilly, was not unpleasant.

Judy had taken the van and gone to the supermarket for the weekly food shopping while I — well wrapped up in a padded jacket and thick jeans, with fingerless gloves and a red woolly hat — was working outside. I was humming under my breath as I planted up hyacinth and narcissi bulbs, standing at a strip of wooden staging outside the shed.

'How's it all going then?' I was so absorbed in my task that I jumped, startled, at the sound of a voice behind me.

Whirling round, I dropped the trowel with a clatter. 'Oh, Bran! I didn't hear you coming.'

'I was rounding up the herd for milking.' He pointed to the stream of cows, their udders swinging, who were making their leisurely way up the field to the milking parlour, with the dog at their heels alert for stragglers. 'Although really they know their own way perfectly well.'

As he casually leaned both forearms on the fence between us, I brushed the soil off my hands and walked across to join him. Seeing him wearing just an open-necked shirt and body warmer over his cord jeans made me feel like a frump in all my wrappings. I whipped off my bobble hat and shook out my hair. It reached almost to my shoulders

109

now; I hadn't had time to get it cut since we came here.

'It's all going well so far,' I said with a smile, then paused as he made some remark about the weather.

I took in a breath and paused. 'Bran, I . . . um . . . about the other evening.' I bent my head and ran a finger along the top rail, avoiding his direct glance. 'You must have thought me . . . er . . . very abrupt and rude when I snapped at you like that.'

'Ah.' He waited for me to go on as I struggled to find the right words, and couldn't. 'Does that mean you've changed your mind?' he said quickly. I raised my head and our eyes met. His held a sort of contained eagerness, and bored into mine as if my answer was supremely important to him.

'Oh, no. Nothing like that.' I shook my head. 'It was just an instinctive reaction. Like Judy says, I always open my mouth first and think afterwards.'

I looked up with a smile and was shocked at the expression of sheer disappointment on his face. His own smile had vanished, and I only just caught the muttered reply as his head drooped and he drummed his fingers on the rail. 'Only the truth is, I'm in a fix, and the situation's getting pretty desperate.'

I looked down at the bowed curly head and had to forcibly restrain my hand from reaching out to stroke those chestnut waves. Out of pure compassion. I suddenly felt really sorry for him, he seemed so downcast.

Instead I glanced at my wristwatch. 'Er, I was just going in for a cup of tea, actually. Would you like one? As an olive branch?' I smiled.

Bran gave a nod and glanced over his shoulder at the disappearing line of cattle. 'I would actually, thanks. Will can get the cows set up. I can spare a few minutes.'

He followed me down the path and we both eased off our wellies in the porch. There was something very personal about seeing him in my kitchen in his socks. Thick grey woolly ones, with a hole in one toe. I wondered again: did he live alone? Who looked after him and didn't darn his socks? I would do my best to find out now we were on our own.

We sat together on the settle with our backs to the window and our feet stretched out towards the warmth of the Rayburn. So close were we that I could smell the fresh, unmistakable scent of his shirt that had been dried in the open air, overlaid with a hint of male sweat.

'So you haven't solved the access problem yet, then?' I picked up my mug and clasped my fingers round it, more for something to do with my hands than for warmth.

'No,' Bran said shortly, 'and I'm not likely to.' He swirled his own tea round and round and gazed into its depths as if the answer lay there. Then, looking up at me, he added, 'But don't think I blame you in any way. Your property is of course your own, to do what you like with.' He cleared his throat and turned towards me. 'The thing is, Jill, I was away from home for several years, and during that time my father became very ill. I didn't know how ill; I was in Argentina at the time, studying methods of rearing beef cattle. And . . . um . . . ' He hesitated and his glance slid away.

'Before that I'd spent three years at agricultural college, travelled a bit with friends . . . ' He paused and his shoulders lifted in a sigh. 'I shall never forgive myself for staying away for so long, but Mother didn't say a lot in her letters and I thought it was only a minor thing. But Dad had contracted sheep-dip poisoning — have you heard of it?'

I nodded. 'I've read about it. It causes dreadful debility and breathing problems, doesn't it?'

'That's right. I had such a shock when I saw him, you'll never believe. He had been such an active man. Now, after so many years when he was unknowingly inhaling toxic fumes, he can't breathe without wheezing and he's so tired all the time, he can hardly drag himself around.' He looked bleakly at me.

'By the time I returned, the farm was terribly run down because he couldn't work it properly, and they'd sold off most of the livestock to make ends meet. We used to breed sheep for market — they'd all gone, and the beef cattle. They'd even sold a couple of fields as well. All that's left now is a small dairy herd and what arable crops we can raise.'

He put down his tea, shrugged and spread his hands wide. 'We can't afford to take on any help except Will, and the fact is, if I can't get this holiday business going, we shall have to sell up completely.'

He swallowed hard and drummed his fingers on the arm of the settle. 'And, Jill — ' He turned tormented eyes to me. ' — that would break my heart. My grandparents had Tregilly before my parents, and I was born here. So you can understand how much it means to me.'

'Of course, and I'm deeply sorry . . . I didn't realise . . . ' My heart went out to him, but equally I was annoyed that he was putting me in this position. Was this a sob story aimed directly at me? As a kind of emotional blackmail, putting me in a position where I felt guilty and selfish for not agreeing to help him out by selling my land?

But no — I'd been studying his expressive face as he was talking, and there was no way he could have been putting on an act. The stress lines across the forehead, the tightness at the corners of his mouth, all combined to convince me his problems were genuine. Which made me feel even worse. I took a breath and opened my mouth to speak.

'Wow, is that the time?' Bran had glanced at the clock and was getting up, hurriedly swallowing the last of his tea. 'Jill, I must go. Thanks for the tea. And for listening.' His eyes probed mine for an instant. 'I'm sorry to run on like that, boring you with my problems.'

'No, no,' I protested, and unthinkingly placed a hand on his arm. 'You're not . . . at all.' I hastily withdrew it, but not before he'd covered it with his own and given me a gentle squeeze. A shock like touching a live wire zinged up my arm, and I swallowed hard as he put the mug down and turned for the door.

'Must go,' he said again. 'I have to pick up my son from school.'

7

His son! I closed the door and leaned back against it. This was a shock. Although why should it be? A charismatic man like Bran was hardly likely to be single. But where was his wife, partner or whatever, if he had to leave his work and collect the child? He'd never mentioned her. Though maybe she had a job too. He'd said how hard-up they were, hadn't he?

I frowned as I picked up the two mugs and made my way across to the sink, still thinking about the little boy. He couldn't be more than seven, because the village school only took infants. And Bran must have been going there, because he was walking . . .

'Oh!' I jumped out of my reverie as the door banged open and Judy burst in, loaded down with carrier bags.

'Phew! That one's heavy!' She dumped

her load on the table and turned towards me. 'The supermarket was *so* busy I thought I was never going to get through. The queues were a mile long.' She ran a hand through her hair. 'Phew, I'm dying for a cup of tea. You?'

As I shook my head, she caught sight of the mugs in my hand. 'Oh, you've had yours already, I see.' She raised an eyebrow. 'Had a visitor?'

'Yes,' I replied casually, rinsing out the mugs. 'Bran was up in the field. I more or less apologised for snapping at him and he came in for a minute.'

'Oh, did he?' Judy looked questioningly at me, waiting for me to expand. But I didn't feel like doing so. For no good reason really. I just wanted to digest all that Bran had told me before I shared it.

'Mm.' I turned towards the door. 'But I must get back. I'm in the middle of planting up all those bulbs we ordered.'

'I'll come and give you a hand when I've put the shopping away.' Judy sank into a chair and cradled her tea.

'Take your time — you need a rest after that marathon.' I smiled over my shoulder and closed the door behind me.

* * *

All through the winter we worked steadily away getting ready for spring, when hopefully we could start selling our plants. The first of our fields was now almost taken up by the poly-tunnels, plus a few rows of daffodil and narcissi bulbs we had planted as infill, thinking we could eventually sell them as cut flowers. Placed invitingly at the gate, they might entice people in to see what else we had to offer. We'd already sold a pleasing number of the potted bulbs in attractive containers that we had put out there before Christmas, so hopefully the word was getting around as to what we were about.

Now it was the middle of January and to our delight, trim rows of green spearheads were showing where we had planted our daffodils and narcissi. Some were even in bud. Before long if the mild weather kept up, we would be picking and hopefully selling them.

★ ★ ★

Then one day I came down from the field humming a little tune under my breath, and expecting to find Judy where I'd left her, at the bottom of the garden. She had been digging up clumps of day lilies and splitting them into smaller pieces. The abandoned spade and tray full of cuttings was there, but of her there was no sign.

Going indoors, I heard her call my name and found her upstairs, kneeling beside her open travelling-bag, with a face the colour of chalk. With drawers and cupboards standing wide open, she was haphazardly cramming clothes and toiletries into it from the pile on the bed, as if her life depended upon it.

'Ju, what on *earth* are you doing?' I

stood transfixed in the doorway, my mouth open.

'Oh, there you are!' She scrambled to her feet and ran agitated fingers through her hair. 'I'm packing. I've had a phone call from a neighbour at home. Oh, Jill — ' She sounded in a terrible state. ' — Mum fell down the stairs and has been taken to hospital. They don't know yet how serious it is — ' She paused for breath. ' — but they asked me if I would come right away. So of course I said yes. There's a train in half an hour and Will's offered to take me to the station.'

'Oh, I'm so sorry!' I grasped her hand and squeezed it, trying to take this all in. Then I frowned. 'Will, you said. Why not me?'

'Oh, I came to the door to call you,' she gabbled, reaching for her dressing gown and bundling it up, 'but you were up in the top field, weren't you?'

'Yes, but . . . ' I nodded, bewildered.

'You didn't hear me. Anyway, Will did, as he was just passing. He must have seen how upset I was, so I told him. He came in to help me look up the train times and he said to be ready in ten minutes.' Judy went on jabbering away as she zipped up the case and reached for her shoulder-bag.

Confronted with this whirlwind of activity, my mind went totally blank. I knew there were a hundred things I needed to say to her, but I could only stammer. 'Is . . . is there anything I can do? Have you got everything . . . ?'

'No, thanks — yes, I think so.' She turned for the door. 'I'm really sorry to run out on you like this, Jill. When we're so busy here too.'

I squeezed her arm. 'Oh, don't be silly. I can manage. I do hope your mum will be all right. Let me know as soon as you can.'

Judy was calling back over her shoulder as she ran down the stairs. 'Of course I will. I'll phone you tonight — or at least, when I know how things stand. By-ee.'

I looked out of the window. Will's car

was at the gate, the engine running. He opened the passenger door as Judy went running down the path. She heaved her bag onto the back seat and they were away.

Stunned, I stood gazing after the car as it disappeared round a bend. Poor Judy — what a shock for her. I nibbled my lip. I couldn't see her coming back very soon. However well her mother recovered, she would take a while to get over the shock, let alone whatever injuries she might have. And Judy, being her only child, would feel it her duty to stay as long as her mother needed her.

I sighed. In spite of what I'd said to Judy, this left me having to cope single-handed for the foreseeable future with all there was to be done here. It was a sobering thought.

However, next day when I woke to a quiet and empty house with no one to talk to, I told myself briskly to stop feeling sorry for myself and just get on with it.

I'd been out to the front to close the gate that had blown open. The wind was freshening and it was banging against the post. While I was there I stopped for a moment to admire our spanking new signboard that was now in place, swinging on its hinges. The colourful and life-like depiction of the two jays was a credit to the sign-writer. It had not come cheap, but nothing of quality ever does.

I tried to ignore the flutterings of fear that were always at the back of my mind when I thought of how much we were spending. When we'd first started here I was so sure my house would soon be sold. I had no idea it would take this long. Maybe I should change estate agents. But if the market was as static as I'd been told, that wouldn't do any good. So my thoughts had run on all through the weeks while we'd been digging, planting, watering, and living in hope. But we were too far advanced with the project now to change our minds, even if pride allowed it.

'Well, well. That looks pretty impressive.'

I was just closing the gate behind me when I heard the familiar voice. My stomach did a leap as usual as I turned to see Bran gazing up at the sign. He was in working clothes with a tall stick in one hand, the dog at his heels.

'Oh, hello, Bran.' I followed his gaze. 'Yes, I thought it was time we advertised what we are, if we expect anyone to buy our stuff.'

'Absolutely.' He bent to hold the dog by the collar as a car drove past, then straightened up. 'You need to be on the internet too, for that. Have you got a website?'

'Website? Oh — no.' I shook my head. 'I'm not very technically-minded. I'd rather be outdoors, grubbing about in the soil.' I smiled. 'Neither of us has the slightest notion how to go about it, and we certainly couldn't afford to pay anyone to set it up for us. At least, not until we really get going and start making a profit.'

'Which you'll do a lot quicker if you're online.' Bran paused and tapped the stick against his leg. 'Um, I could do it for you, if you like.'

'*You* could?' I felt my brows shoot up as I looked at him in surprise.

'Oh, yes.' He nodded. 'I'm quite handy around computers.' I raised an eyebrow. No false modesty there. 'We had to be when I was at college and I've found it very useful since.'

'But — but, like I said, we can't afford . . . '

He raised a dismissive hand. 'Oh, don't worry about that. I'll do it for a cup of coffee — and maybe a bar of chocolate!' He grinned endearingly like a mischievous schoolboy and added, shamefaced, 'I'm a pig for chocolate.'

I smiled absently while my mind was whirling. Although part of me was saying no, no, I don't want to put myself in this man's debt, considering the circumstances, the other half was saying yes, yes. Being online was the modern approach to business, and Bran was right, we should be in on it.

So I stood there in a quandary, hesitating until I was forced to make some kind of reply. 'That's a really kind offer,' I managed, while at the same time my suspicious mind was ticking over non-stop. Why was he doing this? Did he have another motive? After the ding-dong we'd had over the land, why should he offer to do me a favour?

'But of course, I'll have to discuss it with Judy first,' I added. Then my hand flew to my mouth as I remembered. 'Oh!'

'What's the matter?' Bran frowned.

'Judy's not here. Her mother's had an accident and she's had to go and look after her. I don't know how long she'll be away.'

'Well, I suppose you can phone her, can't you?' He shrugged and arched an eyebrow.

There was no denying that. I took a deep breath. 'Yes, of course. Although I don't really want to bother her while she's dealing with this crisis.' I nibbled a thumbnail. 'But I know she would agree. So, if you're really sure, then thank you . . . that would be a huge help.'

'Of course I'm sure. It won't take very long. I'll drop round this evening, shall I?'

'Tonight? Oh, er, yes, all right.' *So soon?* I thought as I nodded and smiled. 'Whenever suits you best.'

Bran twirled the stick in his hand. 'Right. I must get back to work. We had to round up a couple of cows, Bess and me. They'd trampled down a piece of the hedge and got out into the woods. It was quite a job to fetch them back; they were having a high old time.' He laughed and spread his hands. 'Then I managed to patch up the gap in the hedge so well, I couldn't get back over it myself! Which is why we're taking the long way round.'

I smiled and thought how pleasant it was to be leaning on the wall just having a chat, like a couple of friends. If only I wasn't always so conscious of the elephant in the corner looming over me whenever I met Bran, I could have been totally at ease with him.

The truth was, I was beginning to get used to having him around. And to gauging his mood by the expressions on his mobile face. The way his eyes crinkled up at the corners when he smiled. The habit he had of running wild fingers through his hair when he felt pressured, leaving it looking like a haystack. And how the colour of his eyes changed with his moods. Dark, brooding and mysterious when he went off into himself. Light and flecked with motes of gold sunshine when he was amused, as he was now. And I knew they could be hard and black as pebbles when he was put out. Yes, Brandon Trelease was getting under my skin, and it irritated me to find it mattered.

★   ★   ★

Bran turned up that evening as he'd promised. Before that, I'd been down to the village and bought a large box of chocolates which was now secreted in a cupboard, ready to give to him when he'd finished. There was no way I was going to be under any obligation to this man, however friendly and helpful he might be. As long as the 'elephant' remained between us, I could never be entirely relaxed around him.

We had installed the computer in a corner of the sitting room, as there just wasn't space for it anywhere else. Bran eased himself into the chair and switched on.

I knew there was no way I could relax while he sat there working. I hovered there behind him for a few minutes, looking down at the back of his curly head and the broad shoulders that seemed to take up every inch of the small space.

'Um, would you rather be left to get on with it without me hanging around, Bran, or is there anything I can do?'

He half-turned. 'Well no, there's nothing you can actually do, but I don't mind if you sit and watch. You'll have to tell me, anyway, what you want as a heading and how to word the whole thing.'

So I pulled up a chair and sat at his elbow. He was wearing a brushed-cotton checked shirt under a blue sweatshirt and smelled of fresh air and laundry that's been dried outdoors. My eyes kept straying to his hands on the keyboard: strong, capable, brown. Hands that were used to hard, physical toil, but with long, tapering fingers sensitive enough for this job as well.

We worked companionably side by side for some time, our talk being purely of the work in hand, until at last the job was done and Bran pushed back the chair with a sigh and stretched out his long legs. 'Right, that's it,' he said with a smile. 'What do you think?'

'Bran, it is *lovely*,' I said with enthusiasm. 'I never dreamt it would be so good. I can't wait to show it to Judy. It looks really professional.'

I wasn't exaggerating. Across the

banner at the top he had made a colourful design incorporating the 'Two Jays' logo with a trail of flowering plants around it; and below, neatly set out, all the information about the business.

'I'm really glad you like it. And I hope it brings in some custom for you.' He ran a hand through his hair, then yawned hugely. 'Sorry, it's been a long day.'

'I'll put the kettle on,' I replied. 'Strong, hot coffee is what you need. That was the bargain, wasn't it?'

Bran chuckled. 'Shan't argue with that,' he replied. Then, rising to his feet, he followed me down to the kitchen.

We sat for a while in the cosy warmth, relaxing with our drinks. I was thinking wistfully how pleasant this would be if we were just friends who could share a chat and a joke together, without all the unseen and unmentioned 'baggage' that hung in the air between us.

At last Bran rose to go, and with many thanks I passed him the box of chocolates. 'Wow! All these — for me?' His eyes widened, and a broad grin crossed his face. 'Thanks a lot, Jill. Bye.' He raised a hand and vanished into the darkness.

* * *

Next morning dawned dry and mild for once, after a spell of drizzly rain, as I walked outside and surveyed what still had to be done. I was slightly cheered by the sight of a shaft of pale sunlight that was showing through the leafless trees, as I made my way up to the fields.

But I was still thinking about the phone call I'd had from Judy last night. Apparently her mother had broken her right arm as well as being badly shaken up, but Judy had discovered that there was more to it than that.

'I asked her how she'd fallen downstairs — did she trip over something, or what? And she looked really guilty, as if there was some reason but she didn't want to tell me about it.

So I persisted and at last it all came out.' Judy paused and I heard her swallow hard before she went on. 'Apparently she's had several fainting fits she didn't tell me about. Didn't want to worry me, she said, but I think she was just too frightened to go to the doctor in case he found something serious.

'So I took her back in there right away, and it's only a minor heart problem. They've given her tablets and now she is *so* relieved, you can't imagine. Her arm's in plaster, of course, and she's obviously handicapped that way; and however much I tell her, I think she's afraid of fainting again.'

'Oh, Judy, I'm so *sorry*. It looks as if she's going to need you around for a fair while yet.'

'Yes, I know. And *I'm* so sorry that I've dropped you in it, Jill — deserting you like this. At our busiest time too.'

'Don't worry about that — you just concentrate on looking after your mum and stay as long as she needs you. I'll manage here.'

Brave words; and with the prospect of getting my helper back here in the near future slim, the thought of all there was to do single-handed was daunting.

I sighed and paused, still deep in thought, leaning my elbows on the gate before I opened it. The air was still, and every sound was magnified. From the brow of the hill came the triumphant cackle of a hen that had just laid an egg and was telling the world about it, followed by the strident crowing of a rooster keeping her in order.

A tractor chugged across the skyline, carrying a bale of hay on the fork-lift in front of it. *Bran*, I thought, *off to feed the cows. With our hay*. The thought gave me a little warm feeling as I watched him vanish into the distance. I felt a smile lift the corners of my mouth as I turned back to my own property.

Our second field was still empty and untouched, waiting to be turned over. Here we would bring on the bulk of our stock, before potting them up and displaying them in the newly cleared garden space that would be open to the public. Shrubs, perennials, maybe fruit bushes . . . my mind ran on as I thought of all the possibilities.

But first of all, the ground had to be cleared. I glanced over it, then bent and fingered the soil. Being on such a slope, the area was well-drained, and even after the few wet days we'd had was quite workable. That was the next job to be done, and soon. Until we had more space in which to plant, there was no way we could have stock mature enough to sell at the time we needed it.

So it was up to me to get on with it. I turned and headed towards the shed where we'd stored the rotavator.

8

On my way up to the shed, I paused to look into the greenhouse and cast an appreciative eye on the young plants coming on in their pots. They were all looking healthy and thriving. In a few more weeks we could start potting them on, ready for sale. Good. I smiled to myself as I unlocked the shed door and with a flip of excitement, reached for the rotavator.

The machine was heavier than I'd thought at first as I dragged it out of the shed; more so as I pushed it up the slope and through the gate into the field. Once there, with my heart in my mouth I bent and gingerly pulled the ignition cord which turned it on, telling myself sternly that of course with this being such a new experience, I was bound to feel a little nervous, although there was nothing at all to be afraid of.

Even so, I jumped back when it emitted a full-throttle roar; and with my heart pounding, I reduced the power to a more gentle hum.

This is OK. I can handle this, I thought as I set it to work on the field; and I gradually began to relax as it trundled along, effortlessly turning over the topsoil and revealing the rich dark loam underneath. I worked it across from side to side of the field, rather than uphill and down, so I would have maximum control; and for a while as we worked in perfect harmony, I even began to develop a fondness for my gallant little helper. I found myself humming tunelessly under my breath as I glanced over my shoulder at the swath of gleaming soil in our wake, and smiled. Over halfway already — this was a doddle.

Fully confident now, I paused for a rest, turning the engine down to a steady purr while I stopped to draw breath for a minute. Putting one hand to my back that needed a stretch, I straightened up and kept the other on the handle of the machine. I smiled to see there was a flock of busy birds working away at the turned soil behind me, making the most of the worms and grubs I'd disturbed. Not quite the huge flocks of crows and screeching gulls that always followed Bran's tractor, but a miniature reflection of it. These were starlings, blackbirds and sparrows, quietly working away in harmony.

My thoughts drifting, I marvelled at how far I'd come from the classroom. My former colleagues would still be battling with teaching, trying to instil knowledge into the heads of rebellious kids who refused to listen and chose to fool around instead. I'd kept in touch with a couple of them and knew that nothing had changed. While here I was, my own mistress, free as one of the birds I was watching.

But this won't do, I told myself sternly. *You've still got to earn a living, woman. Get on with it.* So I left the birds and my thoughts behind me and carried on up the hill.

After a while I felt my shoulder beginning to ache from guiding the machine around on the turns, but I was loath to stop for another rest as it was going so well. We were nearly at the top now, but the turns were getting more frequent as the field narrowed.

Also, the lie of the land was getting steeper, and there were some large stones along the edge, too big for me to move. I must avoid them at all costs. I bit my lip, stopped humming and concentrated all my attention on the job, bracing myself for the next turn as the machine approached the largest boulder.

I was nearly round when it happened. Suddenly distracted by a loud shout of 'Look out!' from behind me, I caught a flutter of movement out of the corner of my eye. I jumped like a startled rabbit and lost all control of the machine. It hit the boulder with an almighty crash and I saw sparks fly at the grinding of metal on stone. Then it turned over onto its side and tumbled into the ditch, taking me with it.

I screamed as the back of my head hit the rock with a sickening thud, then everything went black as I passed out.

* * *

When I came partially round, I had a vague sensation of being lifted, of being carried in strong arms up and away, my cheek rubbing against soft wool as we went along. Wool that held the faint scent of male sweat. Of the click of a latch as we paused. My rescuer was opening a door and shouting. Then I was being gently lowered face-down onto a bed or a couch, while over and above me urgent voices were chattering. Women, a man, a child's shrill piping.

'Who's that lady? Is she dead?'

'Hush, Ricky. Go outside and play, or help Granddad pick up the eggs . . . '

'Bran, is she that there young lady from down below? Oh, my lor' . . . What's the matter with her?'

'It's her head — look, she's bleeding, poor soul . . . Had we better send for an ambulance . . . ? Wait, Marie — go and get some warm water to bathe it . . . and a towel . . . '

I heard all this vaguely, in a daze; then as someone dabbed the back of my head with a cloth, I screamed and started up, snapping fully awake as a tide of pain surged through me.

'It's all right, my handsome,' came a soothing voice in my ear as a hand pushed me gently back on my side onto the cushion. 'I'm trying not to hurt you, but we must get this cleaned up. You've a nasty cut just here, right on the back of your head; but it's not all that deep, just bleeding a bit. Which is good — that will help to clean it from the inside. Nearly done now . . . '

I couldn't see the speaker, but she gave me the impression of being a motherly figure who had done this sort of thing many times before and was not inclined to panic. I took a deep breath and began to relax.

'There, I think the bleeding's stopped already. You take hold of this here and just hold it against the wound for a minute in case it starts again.' She handed me a piece of cotton wool and I took it with shaking fingers.

I slowly turned over and eased myself into a sitting position, closing my eyes as the room swam around me. As soon as I stopped moving, however, it came back to normal, and I was blinking into the smiling face of a capable-looking middle-aged woman, exactly as I had imagined her to be.

I returned the smile with my own wobbly one, and she patted my arm. 'How does it feel now?'

'O-oh. It aches.' I bit my lip as a stab of pain shot through my head. She gathered up the bowl of water and the stained cloth and turned to leave. 'And thank you,' I called after her. 'But who . . . who are you, please? And where am I?'

Then the door opened, Bran burst in and I knew. 'How . . . ?' he began, then caught sight of me. 'Oh, Jill, you've come round!' He came forward and crouched at my side, reaching for my hand and giving it a squeeze as a frown of concern creased his forehead. 'I — that is, *we*'ve been so worried. I called for an ambulance, and the paramedics are on their way. How are you feeling now?'

'Apart from a splitting headache, not too bad. A bit woozy too.' Very conscious of the feel of his hand in mine, I tried to summon up a smile, and winced.

At that moment the door opened and another woman edged her way round it. Not Bran's mother. Definitely not. She was young — well, about my own age — and very attractive. Slightly built and neatly dressed in slim jeans and a pink sweater beneath a flower-sprigged apron, she had the figure of a dainty doll. Dark hair waved around the perfect oval of her face, pearl drop-earrings swung below, and now focussed curiously on our joined hands were a pair of startlingly blue eyes, the brightest blue I'd ever seen.

Bran withdrew and rose to his feet as I continued staring. My jaw had dropped; I couldn't take my gaze off her. And a slither of ice trickled down my spine. So this was his wife, partner or whatever.

'Bran,' called this vision, 'the paramedic's here.' She stood back to admit a sturdy man in uniform who strode across the room towards me.

'Hello there. I'm Tony.' He held out a hand and clasped mine, then turned and did the same to Bran. 'What's happened to this young lady, then?'

'I had an accident with a piece of machinery and fell backwards. I hit my head on a stone,' I spoke up and answered for myself. The feeling that I was being treated as an object to be talked about rankled.

'Ah. Let's have a look.' He turned my head sideways and parting my hair, gently probed the wound. I stiffened and flinched. 'Sorry, but I have to make sure it's clean. But that looks fine. You can turn back again.' He drew out an instrument and peered into my eyes. 'Mm. No concussion there; that's good.' He straightened up. 'I think you'll be okay, my dear. Rest is what you need, keep warm, and I recommend a hot drink now that we're sure there's no concussion. You're in shock, and will be for some time, but I see you're being well looked after.'

He turned to Bran. 'Your wife should be fine, Mr. Trelease, but if she does feel sick at all, or starts having double vision, don't hesitate to contact your doctor.'

Bran's glance had caught mine and behind the man's back he gave me an embarrassed grin as he arched an eyebrow and shrugged broad shoulders. But the moment had passed and it was too late to correct the mistake now.

Over his shoulder, however, I noticed Marie's face change. The blandness of her expression had suddenly vanished. Now she was gazing at me with an icy look of what appeared to be dislike. Surprised, I held her gaze. Then the hardness disappeared as quickly as it had come. Had I imagined it? Was I being neurotic? I didn't think so, even in my present state of woolly-mindedness.

'That *is* good news.' Bran heaved a sigh as he drew up a footstool and perched at my side. 'You'll soon be okay again, Jill. Phew, thank goodness. When you think what might have happened, you seem to have got off quite lightly.'

'I can't actually remember a lot about it after I landed in the ditch.'

'Oh, I was crossing the field and saw you with the machine. From where I was standing, you seemed to be getting closer and closer to that boulder. I started to run to warn you — ' He raised both hands, palms up. ' — but you'd crashed before I could get there. I doubt you even heard me, did you?'

'*Heard* you?' I shot up in the seat, forgetting, and gasped. Ignoring the pain, I glared at him. 'Of course I heard you! It was *because* you made me jump that I ran into the stone. It was all your *fault*! I was being so careful. And I was perfectly on course to avoid it until then. Bran, how *could* you . . . ?' And to my everlasting shame, I started to cry. Huge tears rolled unchecked down my face. I sobbed from weakness and from shock. From what I saw as Bran's idiocy, from frustration at being left to cope with the business alone, from worry over our financial situation. I wept for my ruined machine, I wept for being so embarrassingly helpless here in a house full of strangers. I wept because I couldn't stop.

Then I became aware that somehow my head had come to rest on Bran's shoulder and that his arm was around me, warm, comforting, wonderful. I sighed, hiccupped and accepted the huge snowy white handkerchief he pulled from a pocket. I mopped myself up and blew firmly into it. It was sodden; I couldn't hand it back now, so I tucked it up my sleeve to launder and return later.

'Better now?' Bran was gazing into my face with concern.

I nodded and sniffed, in no hurry to move or to break this contact, mad at him though I was.

Then Marie came back in. Bran couldn't have seen the expression on her face as she took in the sight of us entwined on the sofa. But I did, and the look she darted at me was pure poison.

It was gone in a second. Was it my imagination again? I didn't think so. But why should she be jealous of me, if that was what it was? What a strange woman. I shrugged off Bran's sheltering arm and sat up.

For the first time I took an interest in my surroundings and looked around the room. I was in a typical farmhouse kitchen. A large pine table stood in the centre, a couple of squashy well-worn armchairs flanked the range, and I was lying on the matching sofa in the window embrasure. The kitchen was homely and full of comfortable clutter.

A large Welsh dresser held patterned china on its shelves. Beneath this, newspapers and farming magazines jostled for space with a plastic tractor and scattered pieces of Lego. It was a family room — unpretentious, welcoming and well-used.

I turned sideways and put my feet to the floor. 'But I must go,' I said. 'I've taken up enough of your time already.' I moved to stand up but my treacherous legs gave way beneath me and I slumped back onto the sofa in a heap. Brave words, but my head was pounding and the movement had left me feeling sick.

'What on earth do you mean, *go?*' Bran's eyebrows shot up. 'You heard what that man Tony said — you've got to *rest.*' His voice rose and boomed in my ear. 'Of course you won't be going home. Not today. Maybe not for several days. You're to stay here until you've completely recovered. There's plenty of room, and Mum's upstairs now getting a room ready for you.' He turned to the younger woman who had said nothing so far, but was watching the scene with an expression of avid interest.

'Go and help her make up the bed, will you, Marie?' She nodded curtly, turned on her heel and left the room.

'Besides which,' Bran said softly into the silence that had fallen, 'it's the least I can do, feeling guilty as I am over causing the accident in the first place.'

'But . . . but . . . ' I said feebly, then looked into his anxious face and sighed. I couldn't go on being mad with him. What was done was done and heaping recriminations on his head wouldn't alter that.

'Well, I am really, really grateful,' I replied, and meant it. The thought of returning to an empty house while I was feeling this rotten was not appealing. 'But I must be keeping you from your work now, surely, aren't I? What were you doing when you came haring down the field after me?'

Bran glanced at his watch, and then at the darkening sky beyond the window. 'Well, actually, yes, I should go and put some stuff away. Will and I were cleaning out the cattle stalls. I'd better go and help him finish, if he hasn't done already. I'll see you later, Jill. And don't try and move from that couch.' He smiled and raised a finger at me as he turned for the door.

Through the window I saw him leave via the back porch, where he exchanged a few words with a stooped figure who was slowly crossing the yard, leaning on a walking stick and pausing every few minutes to draw breath. His father presumably. I remembered Bran saying how he suffered from a chronic lung condition and any exercise led to difficulty with his breathing.

I jumped at the click of the kitchen door opening and turned my head to see who had come in, and saw a little boy hesitating on the threshold. This must be the child I'd heard briefly, but not seen, when Bran had first brought me here.

'Gran?' he called, looking round the

room. Then his face straightened as he realised I was the only person there.

He paused for a moment, shifting from one foot to the other, until I said, 'Your Gran's upstairs,' and smiled at him.

As he slowly crossed the room, regarding me solemnly, I thought what a beautiful child he was. Huge brown eyes in a little pointed face. Bran's eyes, but edged with long lashes that any girl would envy, he had a mop of dark curls and skin of smooth honey-gold.

Still staring at me, he said, 'Hello. Are you feeling better?'

'Yes, I am, thank you. You're Ricky, aren't you?' He nodded slowly. 'I'm Jill and I live in the house at the bottom of your Daddy's field.'

'I know.' He edged a little closer. 'I've seen you and the other lady when I've been going to school. You've got a pretty garden.'

'Yes, that's right. Do you help your daddy and granddad on the farm when you're not in school?'

His face brightened. 'Oh, yes. I ride on the tractor sometimes.' He crossed to the dresser and picked up his toy. 'This is my tractor. It's red, just like Daddy's. Look.' He held it up for me to inspect.

'So it is. Lovely. But I can hear your mummy calling you. She's upstairs too. I think you'd better go.'

The little boy frowned and a bewildered look crossed his face. 'My mummy?' His gaze faltered and he bit his lip. 'Oh, no. That's only Marie. She helps Gran, and she looks after me too.' He shuffled his feet and murmured, 'Because I haven't got a proper mummy.'

9

Eventually I was forced to spend two nights at the farm, itching as I was to get back home. But I must have been more in shock than I realised at first. I couldn't turn my head without feeling dizzy, and trying to stand had me lurching about and clutching at furniture to steady myself.

Bran's mother was a dear, going out of her way to make me feel comfortable and welcome. Not so Marie. Although on the face of it she was perfectly pleasant, there was a certain coldness about her that made me think she was putting on an act. I wondered why she had come to work here in the first place. She was the last sort of person I would have imagined living on a farm. Her painted fingernails, the long skirts she liked to wear, and her elegantly coiffed hair all shrieked 'townie' to me.

And I also wondered how she managed to survive Mrs. Trelease's pasties and hearty stews without adding any weight to her dainty figure.

One night I awoke with an urgent need to go to the bathroom. Swearing under my breath as I reached for my slippers and dressing gown, I stood up too quickly and staggered as my head started whirling. Trying to ignore it, I paused for a minute for it to settle before crossing the room.

The bathroom was on the ground floor, having been built on as an addition to the old house when it was modernised. I tried not to make a sound as I tiptoed down the stairs in the almost-dark, trying to remember exactly where it was. The last thing I wanted was to disturb the household.

But I miscalculated how many stairs there were, stumbled on the last one and clutched frantically at the newel post to steady myself, while one foot caught the edge of the dog's tin feeding bowl and sent it flying across the passage with a clatter.

Horrified, I went rigid, waiting in the lengthening silence. I began to relax, thinking I'd got away with it. But as I stood there I noticed there was a thin streak of light around the edge of the kitchen door. I groaned. Somebody was still up, and now the door was opening.

A tall, dark figure was coming down the passage towards me. 'Oh, Bran,' I whispered, 'it's me.' Instinctively I grabbed at the belt of my robe, which was swinging open, and fastened it.

'Jill! I thought you were an intruder.' His voice was gruff and his expression in the half-light inscrutable as he came towards me. I could, however, see he was clad only in jogging bottoms and was bare-chested. 'What are you doing? Are you all right? Did you need something?' He put a hand under my elbow and guided me towards the kitchen. Snatching up a baggy T-shirt from a chair, he swiftly wriggled into it, with the same awareness I'd felt. I caught a glimpse of broad shoulder muscles rippling down the long back to taper into a narrow waist. The pants were slipping to his hips as he moved and I tore my gaze away before he caught me staring.

'Oh, I'm so sorry. I was on my way to the bathroom and I tripped on the stairs.'

'Are you hurt?' The grip on my arm tightened and he brought his face close to mine. I shook my head and winced as the wall moved.

'No, not at all.' Bran led me to the sofa and lowered me gently into it. 'Do you think anybody else heard me?'

'I shouldn't think so, or they'd be here by now.' He bent and opened the door of the range to poke up the embers. A comforting warmth began to creep through me and I had just started to relax when I was reminded why I'd come down in the first place. 'I must just . . . ' I murmured, getting up again and crossing the room.

When I returned from the bathroom, I found that Bran was sitting on the sofa with his long legs stretched out to the warmth, sipping a steaming mug of coffee. Another mug on my side was waiting for me.

'Yours is cocoa,' he said as I picked it up and gave it a sniff. 'Better for you in your state than tea or coffee.'

I glanced up and thanked him, surprised at his thoughtfulness. Now I noticed that the big table in the centre of the room was littered with papers, notebooks and document files and also, on a spike, what looked like a pile of bills. I could see the tradesmens' headings on them.

As Bran stretched out his feet, thrust into backless leather slippers, his shoulder rubbed against mine and I flinched. To move away would seem too pointed, so I tried to ignore his proximity as all the hairs on my arm rose and quivered. Also, his jogging pants had risen as he stretched out his feet. I swallowed and tore my gaze away from those long brown legs — absently I noticed they were covered in fine dark hairs — and glanced at the clock. 'Bran, it's two in the morning. Why are you still down here?'

He heaved a sigh and ran a hand distractedly through his hair. 'I was going through the accounts and trying to work out exactly where we stand financially. I didn't notice how late it was.'

'Do you really have serious problems, then?' Privately I thought he must have, to be working so late into the night. His face was pale and drawn, with the cleft between the eyebrows starkly etched.

He nodded. 'Until recently I've been just managing to keep us afloat, but now with EU rulings and all this health and safety business — well, we need capital to carry out both repairs and to bring existing equipment up to date.' A frown deepened the cleft on his forehead. 'I'm sure while I was away that Dad deliberately kept from me how bad things actually were. Then when I came back I was thrown in at the deep end. There was only me, as by then

Dad was too ill to cope. It was such a shock, Jill.' He slowly shook his head, and my heart went out to him.

'Mm, it must have been,' I murmured in sympathy.

'I spent my days out in the fields at that time, salvaging what I could. I sold a lot of the livestock, only keeping enough to breed from.' He sighed and lifted his palms. 'If it wasn't for Mum, I'd sell up and leave. Find somewhere smaller to live, get a job. But it would be the end of her if she was forced to move out. She was born on this farm, you see, and has never lived anywhere else.' Bran's brooding eyes met mine. 'Dad worked for her parents, and when he and Mum got married he just moved in.' He glanced around the room. 'I love the place too, and I'd like to think I could keep it on for Ricky.' He sighed. 'But as my parents never had any other children, there's only me to cope with everything.' He rubbed red-rimmed eyes.

'It must be a huge responsibility,' I said softly.

Bran nodded. 'That's why I want to convert the barns. I can get a loan for that, as they're pretty well certain to bring in a profit. But of course, I need access. So it's back to square one.' He shrugged the broad shoulders touching mine.

His mention of the child had given me an opening for the question I was burning to ask. This moment of closeness and the silence of the night made it the perfect time for confidences. It was now or never. Such a chance was unlikely to come again.

'Um, yes, Ricky,' I started hesitantly. 'He's a nice kid.' I drew in a breath. 'I was wondering about . . . about . . . his mother not being around. I know it's none of my business, but . . .'

'Ah.' Bran was looking down at his hands, clasped on his knees, so I couldn't read his expression. 'Ricky's mother was Lola,' he began softly. 'We met in Argentina when I was staying at her father's cattle ranch. She was beautiful — all flashing black eyes and long, swirling hair. I was crazy about her, and I thought she felt the same.' He sighed. 'Very soon we were married, and not long afterwards Lola became pregnant. Then Ricky was born.' He paused and nothing broke the silence but the small noises of the fire. Bran raised his head and let his hands hang loosely between his knees. His eyes met mine and my heart turned over at the sadness and hurt there was in his. 'There were complications after the birth and . . . Jill . . . she died.'

'Oh, Bran, I'm so very sorry,' I murmured. It was inadequate, but what else was there to say?

'Of course, Lola's parents wanted to keep Ricky there with them, but they were both old people. Lola was the youngest of their several children, born late in their lives. So I objected strongly and told them I wanted to bring up my son myself. After all, he's the only part of his mother I have left.' His shoulders lifted in a sigh. 'They saw reason in the end, and I told them they were welcome to come over here and visit any time, but they never did. And I said I would bring Ricky to see them when he was older. But eventually we lost touch. I never hear from them now. And I've never looked at another woman since.'

'Oh Bran, how tragic. I'm so sorry,' I said again, but this time I reached out a hand to him in sympathy, not expecting him to react as he did. But he grasped it in his own and gave it a gentle squeeze, keeping it there long enough for me to feel my body clench in such a tug of desire that I gasped. I told myself sternly it was a long time since I'd felt the touch of a man. That was why I was overreacting.

'Bringing him here was the best thing I ever did,' Bran murmured. 'Now Ricky's the light of my life, and his grandparents adore him. Marie and Mum look after him very well. I don't know how we'd manage without Marie.' Gazing into the fire, he shrugged and sighed.

'She came to us after her parents died. She was their only child, born late in life, and had been looking after them for years. Then when she was left alone, she needed a job and company, so we took her on. Mum thinks the world of her, and she *is* good with Ricky.' He spread his hands. 'But I know he feels the lack of a real mother, especially since he started school and found he's different from the other children. Of course they ask him questions and he doesn't know what to say. I've told him a little bit about his background, but he's too young to really understand.' He turned his haunted eyes to mine again. 'Jill, how do you explain *death* to a six-year-old child?'

What a heartbreaking story it was. If only I could tell Bran how much I sympathised with him. And how much I wanted to throw my arms around him in a comforting hug.

A small silence fell, broken only by the crackling of the fire as we each sank into our own thoughts. I was facing the door we had come through, which had a glass panel in its upper half, partially obscured by a net curtain. Then I was suddenly startled out of my reverie as I caught a glimpse of a shadowy figure pause and look in, before passing behind it and out of sight.

'Bran — ' I jerked my hand away to point. ' — there *is* someone else about. I saw him, or her, through the glass.'

Bran started up and flung the door open, looking down the passage and up the stairs. I heard him pacing the length of the house until he came back, lifted his shoulders and opened both hands in a shrug. 'Not a sign of anyone, or a sound.' He shook his head. 'It must have been the shadow of the trees outside. The moon's rising and there's quite a breeze blowing. That must have been what you saw. It's the only explanation.'

I smiled and made some comment. But I knew what I'd seen and it certainly wasn't a tree.

'But we must get to bed if we're

going to be fit for anything in the morning.' Bran began gathering up his papers and stacking them neatly.

'Yes,' I replied quietly, 'and I'm sorry I disturbed you.'

'Don't be,' he said and his glance lingered on my face. 'It was good to have some company. In the dead of night problems always seem to be twice as bad as they are, don't they?'

'Er — yes.' I paused and dragged my gaze away from his. 'Well, um, good night then, Bran.'

'Good night, Jill. Sleep well.' And to my astonishment, he bent his head and dropped a brief kiss on my cheek.

I left him packing up his work. And all the way up the stairs I kept my hand over the warm spot where his lips had rested.

★　★　★

Next morning I was feeling well enough to go home. The dizzy feeling had vanished and apart from a certain tenderness around the wound, I was completely back to normal; anxious, too, not to impose any longer on the kindness of this family, and to get back to my own home that I'd abandoned so abruptly.

I vaguely remembered, through my haze of pain at the time, giving Bran my door key to lock up the house and make sure everything was all right there. What a lot I owed him and his family. I would have to make it up to them in some way.

My thoughts were running on along these lines as I moved about my room, packing up and stripping the bed, when I half-turned and found Marie in the doorway, watching me.

'Oh, you've done that already,' she said, coming forward and bending to pick up the bed linen. 'I'll get these in the wash then.'

'Oh, thanks,' I said absent-mindedly. I was glancing out of the window where I could see Bran, hand in hand with Ricky on the way to school. The child was skipping along, talking animatedly, as Bran bent his head to listen to the little boy's prattle.

'Bran adores Ricky, doesn't he?' I remarked. 'He was telling me about his background. Isn't it sad?'

She straightened and gave me a sharp look. 'Ricky doesn't remember anything about his mother or about Argentina, so no, it isn't sad. He's very happy here with his father and us. He certainly doesn't need *you* to feel sorry for him.'

Her tone of voice was so aggressive that I stopped what I was doing and just stared at her. Marie was glaring back at me, clutching the bundle of linen tightly to her chest. Beneath a demure overall she was wearing a flounced skirt today, slightly Spanish-looking, with a peasant-style cotton blouse and several necklaces and rings as well as the ear bobs.

I felt my eyes widen in surprise. 'It's only because Ricky was telling me he didn't have a 'proper mummy', so of course I felt sorry for him. And Bran said he feels different from the other children now he goes to school.'

'Hah! That would have been last night, I suppose, wouldn't it?' Bright flags of colour appeared on Marie's cheeks now as she glowered at me.

I flinched at the virulence in the woman's voice and took a step back as she advanced, waving a finger in my face. 'I suppose that was why you were both sitting in the kitchen at two o'clock in the morning,' she hissed, 'holding *hands*!' She was wringing a pillowcase round and round now, as if she wished it was my neck. 'And don't even try to deny it. I *saw* you. When I heard a noise and came down to see what it was.'

In case you missed something, more like, I thought. But I wouldn't stoop to her level and start a slanging match. Aloud I said bitterly, 'You've got it all wrong, Marie. But you wouldn't believe there was a perfectly innocent reason for that, would you?'

'Too right I wouldn't,' came the retort.

'In that case I won't even try to explain.' I turned my back to her, picked up the duvet and gave it a good shake, more calmly than I felt.

'I've seen you making eyes at Bran,' she muttered. 'Don't think I haven't. Cuddling up with him on the sofa after you bumped your head. Making the most of it. Playing up to him for all it's worth.' She scowled at me and stalked across the room, then half-turned on her heel and stabbed a finger in the air again. 'But you needn't think it'll get you anywhere. We're a very happy family up here, just as we are, so don't think you can worm your way in and spoil it.'

I was left speechless for a moment at this totally unwarranted attack, before I gathered my wits enough to reply. My voice was as icy as I could make it as I stared her down. 'I wasn't aware, Marie, that you *were* one of the family. I was told you were the paid help.'

Lost for words for a moment, she stood goggling at me, her mouth opening and closing like a fish. But with me, the penny had dropped. She wanted Bran for herself and saw me as an intruder. That made perfect sense — it accounted for her animosity that had surprised me so much, and explained a few other things such as why she had made herself indispensable to Mrs. Trelease, whom I'd overheard several times singing her praises. The woman was hoping to get at the son through the mother. I could see through her deviousness now and it stunned me.

'For goodness' sake, Marie,' I went on, 'are you *jealous?* Of me?' I could hardly believe it. She glowered and gave me another vicious look.

'Just keep away from Bran, that's all,' she spat. 'He's had enough trouble in his life without you adding to it.'

I saw red then and let fly at her. 'You're all sorts of a fool if you think there's anything going on between Bran and me.' I hurled the duvet back on the bed and, hands on my hips, glared back. 'He told me himself he's finished with women. Period. So you are completely overreacting, Marie. You haven't a chance with him, if that's what you're trying for.' I tossed my head and paused for breath. 'And even if there *was* anything between Bran and me, it's absolutely none of your business.' Seething, I couldn't resist one final dart as I turned to leave. Over my shoulder I added, 'And that's not to say I wouldn't *like* there to be, either.'

So think about that one, you witch. I was so churned up with conflicting emotions I ran all the way downstairs, fighting against tears. For I'd obviously made an enemy, and I hated to fall out with anyone.

10

As soon as I had settled in at home, I called Judy and told her all that had happened. She was horrified as I recounted the story of my accident, and I could imagine her expression as she wailed down the line.

'Oh, Jill, you could have been killed! Whatever possessed you to think you could handle that machine on your own?'

I bit my tongue to prevent myself flaring up and protesting that I had been managing perfectly well until . . . well yes, better to leave Bran out of this. It would only sound like telling tales.

'It had to be done, Ju,' I replied in a level tone. 'We have to get that ground planted up, and soon.'

'And I'm feeling so guilty at not being there to help. I'm letting you down terribly.' There was a catch in her voice.

'Oh, don't be silly. You can't be in two places at once,' I reassured her. 'Anyway, how is your mother now?'

'Much better in herself. She seems to have got her confidence back now she can see the tablets are working.'

'Oh, that's good. I'm so glad for you both. So it's just her arm now, is it?'

'Yes. Yes, that's right. And she's also getting more confident at coping with that lately.' She paused. 'In fact, I'm wondering if I might be able to come down soon — just for a few days, it would have to be — and give you a hand. I'd have to go back of course, but . . . it would make me feel better if I could help things along a bit down there.'

'Oh, Judy, that would be marvellous! Are you're sure?'

'I think so. Mum's got a new friend from down the road who she met at the W.I. She's a nice person who's offered to pop in every morning and see if she's all right. I could leave ready-meals for her, and . . . well, I think it should work. Just for a short while, as I said.'

'Oh, fantastic! Have you any idea when you might be coming?'

'As soon as I can. I've been casually dropping hints to Mum over the past few days, so it wouldn't come as a shock to her. Now I can be more definite and I'll aim for next Monday, unless anything comes up in the meantime.'

'Great, I'll look forward to it and get the bed aired!'

'Lovely. I'm longing to see how things in the nursery are getting on.'

'You'll be surprised. There are green shoots everywhere, and loads of the daffodils are in flower.'

'Already? And it's still only January. We've had frosts and icy roads here for the past week.'

'Couldn't be more different down here. Mild and drizzly, that's us. Anyway, see you soon, Ju. Bye now.'

I put down the phone with a smile on

my face. The promise of help had cheered me more than I'd realised, and I hummed a little tune under my breath as I went outside to see what had changed since I'd been away.

It had only been two days, but I could see what a spurt the bulbs had put on, and there was even a clump of primroses in flower at the bottom of a hedge.

I walked up to the perimeter where the post and rail fence separated our land from Bran's. I could hear the thrum of the tractor and noticed that Will was up at the top end of the field and had started ploughing. The cattle were now contained behind a newly erected wire fence with a makeshift gate in it that divided the field in two. Perhaps Bran was going to plant up the top part with cauliflower this season, or maybe a cereal crop.

My thoughts wandering, I leaned on the fence, idly watching the tractor circling round and thinking how easy it looked, compared with my own amateur effort that had ended in such grief.

I was brought abruptly back to the present, however, when I realised that the whole fence was moving under my weight, and I found that one of the posts had worked loose and was coming out of the ground. Several of the rails on each side of it were wobbly as well.

Straightening up, I investigated the bottom of the post and discovered not only had it come loose, but it had rotted through and would have to be replaced. I bit my lip in annoyance. What a nuisance. Another job to be done. One I wouldn't be able to do myself either, even with Judy to help. I had absolutely no idea where to start. So it would have to wait until I could find a carpenter. I sighed. More expense.

I spent the rest of the morning picking and bunching daffodils and narcissi, which I put in buckets at the front gate, hoping to sell them to passers- by. Not that the general public came this way much. It was a quiet by-road and only if people who lived along it were going to the village would they pass our gate.

By evening I'd only sold one or two bunches. This would not do. I had to make the most of what flowers we did have. There were too many to go to waste, but not enough to send up to Covent Garden as the big growers did. No, I must find another way.

Next morning I gathered up my stock, put it in the car and drove down to the village. The local shop sold pretty much everything, as is the way in rural villages, so I would see if they'd take my flowers. I'd been in the store several times before and found the Bryants, the husband and wife team who ran it, pleasant and friendly. Yes! They would be pleased to take the daffs and anything else I liked to bring them in future.

We came to an amicable arrangement and I left the shop with a spring in my step and a smile on my face. The profit

I'd get would be only a drop in the ocean by the time they'd taken their cut, but at least it was something, and the display would also be a good advertisement for the business.

Before returning home, I wandered down the street to have a glance at the river for a change of scenery and also to get some fish for lunch from the shop on the quay nearby.

I had to pass the school on the way, where the children were lining up to go inside, and the parents were just leaving. I noticed Bran was among them and my heart gave the usual irritating leap as he saw me and raised a hand. He was wearing a chunky red cable-knit sweater and jeans, his hair lifting in the slight breeze blowing off the water.

'Jill! Hello.' He stopped and looked me appraisingly up and down. 'How are you now? No recurrence of the headache?'

'No, not at all.' I smiled. 'I'm perfectly fine now. In fact, I was going to call in at the farm later. I've got some flowers in the car for your mother, to thank her for her kindness to me. And Marie as well, of course,' I hastily added. 'Now I can give them to you instead.'

'Oh, right.' He gave a lazy smile and rocked back on his heels. 'Well, I've had an idea.' He nodded towards the small café on the quay that apparently stayed open all year round. A woman was busy sweeping at the open door, from where a delicious smell of frying bacon was drifting out. 'Have you got time to stay on for a minute?' He arched a brow. 'I could buy you a cup of coffee as an apology for causing your accident in the first place. And I'm dying for a bacon sandwich. I didn't have time for breakfast this morning.'

'Oh! That would be lovely, Bran, thank you.' My mouth had already started to water at the thought of bacon. My own breakfast had been a snatched piece of toast in my hand as I wandered up to the field.

Minutes later we were seated in the window of the café, overlooking the tranquil river. An early mist was rapidly dispersing and pale fingers of sunlight were poking through the haze. A couple of pure white egrets were poking about in the mud near the shore, while standing patiently in the reeds I could make out the figure of a motionless grey heron. Beyond, on the other side of the water, stunted oak trees, leafless now, swept down to the shore, with a bank of green fields rising steeply behind them.

'A sandwich for you too?' Bran turned to me as the waitress hovered.

Throwing all thoughts of calories to the wind, I nodded. 'Yes, please. My breakfast was so early I've forgotten I had one.'

Bran grinned and gave the order, and we sat munching in companionable silence for a few minutes. Then, following my line of sight, Bran pointed a finger down river. 'Actually, I own a useless patch of land further on round that bend.'

Surprised, I smiled and turned towards him. 'You do? Oh, why is it useless?'

'Because it's nothing but marsh and mud now. Not fit for anything. It's a hangover from way back, when there was a lot of mining activity around here.' He shrugged and stirred his coffee. 'You'd never believe it now, but quite big ships used to come up on the tide, taking the tin and copper ore out and bringing in timber and coal for the mines. It was a really busy place.'

I followed his pointing finger. 'I'd never have guessed it from here.'

'No. It was a long time ago.' Bran sipped his drink and looked at me over the rim. 'But one of my ancestors was into mining in a big way, and had a quay built for his business. You can just see the remains of it, and other ancient artefacts, if you know where to look. There were several small quays up and down the river, and masses of machinery, all derelict and overgrown now.'

We fell silent again, each lost in our own thoughts, watching the activity on the river. Not that there was much going on. A couple of small fishing boats drifted past, presumably after the oysters and mussels that abounded locally. Colourful leisure craft had been hauled out of the water and were laid up on the quay, waiting for the season to begin. Seagulls were screeching and fighting for food scraps among the cast-up wrack on the shore.

Bran and I were sitting on opposite sides of the table and I was studying his profile as he looked out of the window. The firm, determined jaw, the straight nose. The mobile, sensitive mouth. It was a face that could have been carved on a Greek statue.

Then he turned suddenly with some remark and caught me staring at him. I felt heat spring to my cheeks as I nodded and hastily turned away.

'Er, do you take Ricky to school every day?' I blurted to cover the awkward moment, then bent my head and picked up my sandwich.

'Whenever I'm not too busy,' Bran replied evenly. 'I like to give him as much of my time as I can.'

'Mm, I can understand that.' I paused. 'I used to teach at one time.' I was stirring my coffee round and round, lost in the past. 'But I couldn't stand the kids. They drove me to distraction and I had to give it up eventually.' I raised my head and was surprised at the expression on Bran's face. He was looking . . . how exactly? It was hard to describe it. Kind of hurt, and sad. Surprised too. But why? What had I said? Absolutely nothing that could have upset him. What an enigma the man was. I shrugged and changed the subject.

'Bran, do you remember that night when we were in the kitchen and I thought I saw a face through the glass? When you told me it must have been shadows of the trees outside?'

'Oh, um, yes. Yes, I do. What about it?' He raised an eyebrow and held my gaze as he finished his coffee.

'Well, next day I discovered it had been Marie looking in. She told me so. Apparently she'd heard the noise I made and came down to see what it was.'

'Oh? Why didn't she come in, then?'

'If you remember, we were holding hands at that point.' I withdrew my gaze from his. 'Bran, she got totally the wrong impression.'

He frowned. 'What do you mean?'

'Oh, come on, think about it!' I chided him. 'Two people in the early hours of the morning, cosying up on the sofa in front of the fire. What do you *suppose* she thought?'

Bran's eyes widened as the penny dropped. 'She thought . . . that I . . . that you and I . . . '

' . . . were having a secret assignation,' I finished.

'But that's preposterous!' he blurted.

'As if I . . . as if we would!' And he burst into peals of hearty laughter.

I pasted the semblance of a smile on my face too, but a small part of me was wishing he hadn't dismissed the idea quite so out of hand. And I refrained from telling him of what had followed in the morning between Marie and myself. It would have been too much like telling tales.

I was sunk so deeply in my own thoughts when we parted that I completely forgot the fish I had meant to buy. And having to turn round and drive most of the way back for it did nothing to improve my mood.

Judy returned the following week as we had hoped, and I drove into Falmouth to pick her up from the station.

'Oh, it's so good to see you!' I exclaimed as we embraced.

'You too.' She gave me a look of concern before we separated. 'Are you sure you're all right now? Your head's completely better?'

'Absolutely.' I unlocked the car and she hefted her bag into the boot. 'Fighting fit and itching to get on with the work — but that's not the only reason I'm so glad to see you,' I laughed. 'I've been missing your company too. It's been quite strange living alone. I've found myself talking out loud sometimes, before I remember and think what a fool I am.'

'Well, I'm glad to be back here for a bit of peace and quiet,' Judy said as we arrived home and she got out of the car. 'The last few weeks have been quite a strain.'

'I can imagine so. What with the worry over your mother, as well as physically looking after her, it must have been very demanding.'

Privately I had noticed how tired Judy was looking, but decided it wouldn't be tactful to say so. She'd lost weight too. Her face was definitely thinner. Reading between the lines, I'd say she'd had a rougher time than she was admitting.

★　　★　　★

'So, what's the first job to be tackled? I've lost track of where we were when I was called away.'

It was the following morning — a welcome dry one although it had gone much colder, and a smattering of hoar frost had sprinkled the hedges overnight. However, there was a hint of sunshine to come which would soon disperse that, and some physical work would warm us up.

We stood surveying our land, Judy with her arms folded around herself for warmth was looking around with interest. 'Oh, you managed to get that piece of field turned over then.'

'Before the accident, you mean. Yes, I'd almost finished, it was so annoying.'

'Well, we can leave that small bit, can't we? It doesn't matter that much. There's plenty of ground ready to be planted up. Are we putting those young shrubs in there? The ones we grew from cuttings?' She turned to me, pointing a finger.

'Yes, that's the idea. They're big enough to come out of the greenhouse now and harden up. When they've grown a bit more, we'll pot them up and display them for sale, along with the perennials.'

We worked solidly all that day and went to bed exhausted, but with a sense of great satisfaction at the sight of our neat rows of trim little plants.

* * *

I had slept so deeply after the tiring day we'd had, that when I heard some kind of rumpus going on outside, it took me some time to come round. Bleary-eyed, I glanced at the time. It was only six o'clock. Whatever was going on?

Then I heard Judy's voice calling my name. 'Jill, wake up! You've got to come — quickly!' She poked a tousled head around my door. 'Get some clothes on. Come outside. Oh my, you'll never *believe* this,' she wailed as she went clattering downstairs.

Rubbing the sleep from my eyes, I pulled on jeans over my pyjamas and grabbing a sweater as I went, hurried after her.

11

Judy was right — I *could* hardly believe the sight that met my eyes. All over our carefully tended land, all over the rows of tender new plants in the field that we'd put in only yesterday, a herd of cows was leisurely grazing. Enormous black-and-white creatures, they seemed in no hurry to move, even when we both went at them shouting, Judy clapping her hands and me waving the biggest stick I could find. But they turned their vast hind quarters round in their own time and ambled back up through the field, switching their tails, trampling over what plants were left, and still munching on the last fragments of their breakfast.

Then we staggered up to the top of the garden. Oh, no! Now I could see what had happened. The piece of post and rail fence I'd not yet had repaired had collapsed completely beneath the animals' weight and now lay useless on the ground.

'Quick, stop up the gap with anything you can find, before they come back,' I shouted to Judy as I ran to the shed for some lengths of scrap wood we'd chucked in a pile when we were turning it out.

Judy had found some bushy branches left in the ditch after we'd trimmed the privet hedge, and together we managed to erect a makeshift barrier that would do for the time being. Then as we looked back at the wreckage of our nursery, tears welled behind my eyes. Heavy hooves had trampled most of the plants into the muddy ground, pats of the animals' mess lay everywhere, and they had even barged into one of the poly-tunnels and made a hole in the side of it.

'Oh ... oh ... *no!*' Judy and I turned and fell into each other's arms. Then our scalding tears flowed, unchecked, for some time.

But the outpouring of emotion was a release of sorts. After that came the anger. And logical thought. These were Bran's cows. I frowned. I could understand that yes, our fence was unsound, and that had been my fault. But how had they got through the top gate in the perfectly solid hedge between his side of the field and the farmyard? Part of me wanted to go storming up there and confront him, but the most pressing need was to assess what damage had been done to our property and how much could be salvaged from the wreckage.

I went to join Judy, who was walking slowly up and down between the rows. 'How bad is it actually? As bad as it looks? What do you think?' I bit my lip and crouched down to examine the plants more closely.

'I think some places are better than others.' She pointed. 'That section is a write-off, where the cows first came through. But down here, look, some of the plants have only been bent over, not broken off. I think we could save those by staking them, don't you?'

'Mm, maybe. But it's only a drop in the ocean. We'll never get back to where we were in time for the season. It's nearly Easter now.' I swallowed down a sob. More weeping would achieve nothing. 'Oh, Ju, we're ruined!' I wailed.

Judy's small white face stared bleakly back at me. Then, suddenly furious, she stamped a foot. 'Well, they're Bran's cows, aren't they? *He*'s responsible for all this!' She flung out her hands. 'How about getting compensation from him? Then if he refuses, we could sue him in the small claims courts.'

I shook my head. 'We couldn't afford to do that. It would cost us. And if we did happen to lose the case, it would cost a whole lot more.'

'Oh, I suppose so.' She nodded and turned away. 'But we must go up there and tell him. Get him to come down and see it for himself.'

'Of course we will.' I glanced down at

my muddy knees and remembered I was still in pyjamas underneath. 'Just as soon as we're decently dressed.'

As we made our way back to the house I walked more slowly than Judy, my mind whirling. Knowing how hard-up Bran was, how could I under the circumstances demand compensation from him? It would probably run into hundreds of pounds to replace all the stock we'd lost, apart from the potential summer sales.

And there was our personal relationship to consider. Apart from having become friends, we were also neighbours and would have to live in close proximity afterwards. But . . . I stopped and turned back to survey the devastation again.

Although we still had left the trays of annual bedding plants that were in the greenhouse, and also in the polytunnels, we'd been relying on the perennial stock outdoors to bring in the money. Which had mostly been trashed. Yes, it was bad, whichever way one looked at it. I sighed as I turned the corner and caught up with Judy.

I was surprised to find her in earnest conversation with Will Taylor, who was leaning over our garden gate.

'Hi, Jill.' He straightened and pushed back the baseball cap that was perched on his mop of straw-coloured hair. 'Judy's just been telling me about the cows. I'm *so* sorry. I can't imagine how it happened.' He spread his huge hands and shrugged. 'That gate's always securely fastened by night.' He shook his head. 'Anyway, I'm on my way to work now, so I'll get Bran onto it and see what we can do.' He turned to leave. 'With your permission, I'll go up through the field and have a look at the damage on the way.'

'OK. Feel free.' I raised an open hand. 'And you can tell him we'll be round to see him very soon.'

'Shall we come with you as far as the fence and show you the worst places?' Judy said, glancing at me.

'Sure.' I nodded and turned to go. At

that moment, however, I heard the phone ringing in the cottage. 'I'll get that and follow you up there,' I said, running into the house to answer it.

The call was from an old friend of mine, one of the staff at the school where I used to teach. Those days seemed like another lifetime now, and I really couldn't get very interested in school news anymore. I cut her off as soon as I decently could. I'd come too far since then and had too much else to think about.

By the time I'd washed and changed out of pyjamas, Judy was back, and she now placed a steaming cup of coffee at my elbow.

'Oh, wonderful.' I smiled at her. 'I guess we both need this.' I took a sip and leaned back. 'What did Will say?'

'He's offered to repair the fence for us.' Judy turned sparkling eyes to me. 'Isn't that kind of him?'

'Oh, yes. Wonderful. That's a relief.' I sighed and summoned up a smile. 'One less thing to worry about.'

'He'll do it later today,' Judy said, tossing slices of bread into the toaster. 'It's a two-handed job,' she added casually, 'so I said I'll help him.'

'*You* will?' I glanced at her in surprise. 'I didn't know carpentry was one of your talents. You've kept that very well hidden.'

To my further surprise, I saw she was actually blushing, before she turned away, adding hastily, 'Oh, I'm only going to hold the wood steady and pass Will the nails — stuff like that. But he said it would be a great help, and two of us could finish the job a lot quicker than he could on his own. Because of course, he has to get back to his farm work as soon as he can.'

My gaze stayed on Judy's back for a while as she busied herself buttering toast and rattling plates. Until her blushes faded? I wondered.

Well, well. I felt my eyes widen. Judy and Will? This was a new development, if my hunch was right. But it fitted.

Judy had never been without someone in her life to lean on. I knew she had found the separation from Hal particularly painful, and having to cope alone had come as a terrible shock to her. No, Judy needed a man in her life, and now it was looking as if she might have found one. I felt a pang of something like envy, and quickly banished it.

But if so, my thoughts ran on, how was this going to affect us and our business? Although we *had* made a pact at the beginning that either of us could pull out if our circumstances changed, I hadn't imagined it would happen so soon. I had a momentary vision of an uncertain future.

Then I drew in a breath and snapped back to the present, smiling at Judy as she turned round and passed me a slice of toast, her face having returned to its normal colour. It was no good looking ahead yet; it might all come to nothing. I could well be jumping to conclusions.

The morning wore on as we went up and down the rows of battered plants, reviving those we could and pulling up the ones that were too far gone. Then I started shovelling up the muck the animals had left. 'At least we've got some free manure,' I joked, tossing it into a heap. If I didn't laugh, I'd start crying again.

And all the time I was working the thought was running through my mind — why hadn't Bran come down to apologise as he ought, even just to see the carnage his animals had caused? Why should I go haring up there to him? Will would have obviously told him by now what had happened. And he hadn't had the decency to show his face. What sort of man *was* he? Silently fuming, I heaved another cowpat onto the pile.

★ ★ ★

When the afternoon came round and Bran still hadn't showed up, I changed my mind. I *was* going up to the farm and have it out with him. I left Judy helping Will with the fence and taking the short cut that meant skirting the field, I entered the farm through the gate that should have been locked, according to Will, but hadn't been. With such disastrous results.

By the time I'd crossed the yard, I was in a raging temper. My cheeks felt flushed and hot and I knew there was a scowl on my face.

Just as I approached the house, however, the Land Rover with Bran at the wheel came roaring up the drive and stopped beside me.

'Oh, *there* you are, Brandon Trelease,' I yelled as he jumped out of the vehicle. 'At last! I've been waiting down there all day for you to show your face.' I jerked my head towards the nursery. 'You do *know* the damage your cows have done, don't you? Will told you?'

'Yes, I know.' Bran leaned on the

half-open door of the vehicle, jingling his keys in one hand. 'And I'm extremely sorry about it, of course.'

My subconscious mind registered how tired he was looking. His brow was puckered and his eyes dull, but I was in no mood to dwell on it.

He slowly shook his head. 'But I've no idea how they got out of the field.' His voice was even and cool. Such a contrast to mine, in fact, that I took a step backwards in surprise.

'It couldn't have been sheer carelessness on your part for not fastening the gate properly, I suppose?' My voice dripped sarcasm as I glared at him. In my mind's eye I could see myself from his viewpoint, and knew I was ranting like a fish-wife. But having started, I just couldn't stop. And why didn't he *argue* with me or at least say something in his own defence?

I saw the frown deepen. His eyes were like black glass as he stared me down, but still he didn't interrupt me.

'So, you knew,' I snapped. 'And you

didn't have the decency to come down and apologise to my face? You had to wait until *I* came to *you?* Well, I call that just sheer bad manners.'

His detachment and refusal to be drawn was irritating me more than if he'd yelled back in return, and for a moment it threw me. I paused and took a deep breath. Looking down at me from his full height, Brandon Trelease was making me feel small and slightly silly for being in such a temper. Which maddened me even more.

'And I take it this attack is an example of perfect manners on your own part?' Bran arched one eyebrow and looked steadily down at my face, making me feel like an insect. 'Of course I fully intended to call round later, but I've been extremely busy today. I've got a lot on my mind at the moment.'

Huh, I thought, looking him up and down. His 'busyness' certainly hadn't been around the farm. That was obvious from his neatly pressed jeans and smart maroon sweater. But he didn't expand any further, only turning to slam the car door and stuff the keys in his pocket.

'And if we're having a slanging match,' Bran went on icily, turning back to me, 'has it occurred to you that by leaving your boundary fence in such a dilapidated state, you were just as responsible for what happened as I am?'

I took a step back as Bran loomed over me with a stabbing finger. He was close enough for me to feel his warm breath on my face. He smelled of peppermint, clean and astringent. As the black eyes bored into my skull, I felt my knees weaken. I had to try hard to stay mad at him. To remember that however this man's charisma was affecting me, he was the cause of my present troubles and probably the ruin of all my hopes and dreams. Then what he had just said sank in.

'But . . . but . . . ' I found myself suddenly floundering at the perfect truth of his remark, which made me more furious than ever. Because he did have a point, of course.

I tried to face down his implacable stare. 'But you've never *put* cows in that part of the field before,' I blurted, 'so of course I didn't rush to get the fence mended. It was only because *your* gate was open. So don't try and wriggle out of it by blaming me!' I knew I was raging as much at myself as at him, but still the wounding words continued to pour out of me.

'Well, the way I see it,' he snarled, 'I've a perfect right to keep cows on any part of my land I want to, without informing *you*.' And he turned his shoulder on me and began to walk away.

I flung my hands wide and glowered at his retreating back, as a hot tide of fury surged through me again. 'But it's all because of *you* we've lost the best part of the young plants we were depending on for our income this summer! We could be ruined!'

He turned once, and glared back over

his shoulder. 'That makes two of us, then,' he muttered, 'according to my bank manager.'

I only vaguely registered what he'd said as, blinded by tears, I turned on a heel, determined not to give way while he was watching. Then what Bran had said suddenly sank in. I stopped on a breath and the rest of my tirade flew out of my head in concern as I really looked at him. Pale and haggard, his back stooped like an old man's, all the usual spring had gone out of his step. I gasped. There was something very wrong.

'Bran, what is it?' I called after him. 'What's happened? You're in trouble, did you say? Oh, I'm so sorry. What's the matter?'

He turned back, glaring at me, his eyes cold, and shook his head. 'I don't want to talk about it.' Tight-lipped, he added, 'Especially to you. So just mind your own business for once, and leave me alone, will you?'

I recoiled and felt my jaw drop. It was

like a slap in the face. I stood rooted to the spot for a long moment staring after him, too shocked to move, as he stalked away and out of sight.

12

Will and Judy had finished repairing the fence by the time I reached them, and as I approached they were deep in earnest conversation. Their backs were towards me and they obviously hadn't heard me coming. It gave me a minute to compose my jangling nerves after the set-to I'd just had with Bran, and to paste a smile on my face.

'So I'll see you on Saturday,' Will was saying, as he picked up his tools and turned to leave.

Then Judy caught sight of me and her face turned bright pink. 'Yes, lovely,' she replied and came to walk beside me back to the house.

'What was that all about? I asked casually. 'What's happening on Saturday?'

Her flush deepened. 'Will's taking me to the cinema. In Falmouth. That new release is on there and you know how I wanted to see it.' Shaking her head, she spread her hands wide. 'I remember you telling me you weren't interested, so I'll be glad of his company. I don't like watching films on my own. He's picking me up at six.'

I couldn't help smiling as she gabbled away, and waited until she stopped to draw breath, before saying, 'You like Will, don't you?'

Avoiding my eyes, Judy nodded. 'Yes, I do. He's a nice person, Jill. Kind and thoughtful.' She turned to me as she added, slightly on the defensive, 'There's a lot more to him than the lumbering great farmhand type he appears to be.'

'I'm sure there is. I haven't really had a chance to get to know him properly.'

'Anyway . . . ' Judy paused as we entered the house. ' . . . what did Bran say about the damage?'

'Er . . . ' I struggled to think of a reply. 'He wasn't very forthcoming, really. I won't say he wasn't concerned, and he *did* apologise.' I spread my hands and shrugged. 'But he gave me the impression that he thought the fault was as much ours as his, because our fence was weak.' It was the truth. However, I didn't tell her how I'd lost my temper and yelled at him, when he had remained so cool. Or, having blown my top and made such a fool of myself, Bran had suddenly taken all the wind out of my sails. Or that I didn't know how I was ever going to look him in the face again.

'So in other words, he chickened out of taking the blame?' Judy's eyes widened as she flared up. 'Huh! The least he could have done was come down and *seen* the mess we're in.'

'That's what I thought,' I replied bleakly. 'But I suppose he might yet, in his own good time.' Hardly likely, I thought to myself, after what I'd said to him.

A couple of days passed as we staked up the damaged shrubs and tidied the ground that had been badly trodden. I was coming back to the house one lunchtime, having left Judy finishing a job in the greenhouse, when I noticed a large van pull up outside our gate. I wasn't overly surprised, as delivery vans for all three cottages usually stopped in the only bit of lay-by there was along the narrow road.

But this carrier had opened our gate and was now going back to the van, to emerge with his arms piled high with several wooden crates that he placed on the step outside our front door.

'Delivery, miss,' he said with a smile as we met. 'Sign here if you will.' He flourished a piece of paper and a pen at me.

'B-but I haven't ordered anything,' I replied, bemused. 'You must have got the wrong address.'

He peered closely at the slip. 'One, Creekside Cottages. Name of Laity?'

I frowned and nodded. 'Yes, that's me.'

'Right.' He thrust the note at me again. I signed it and vaguely thanked him as I wondered what on earth was in the crates, and where they had come from. Perhaps Judy knew, but surely she wouldn't have ordered anything without telling me.

I bent and removed the lid of the first box. Plants! I glanced briefly inside the other two. Three crates of young shrubs, looking very similar to the ones we'd lost to the cows. My stomach did a flip as light began to dawn. I grabbed at a card stuck on the inside of the lid and ripped it off.

It was signed with a large 'B.'

* * *

Oh, my god! Bran! After all I'd said and thought about him, he'd done this. Quietly, unassuming, in spite of his own problems. In such a contrast to my own loud-mouthing of him. Stunned, I stood riveted to the spot, biting my lip until it bled, as my mind whirled. Thinking back to how I'd lost my temper, how I'd yelled at him, how I'd made an utter fool of myself. And how I would have to grit my teeth now and take myself up to the farm. Swallow my stiff-necked pride, apologise and thank him . . . It was not going to be easy.

At that moment Judy came around the corner and seeing the boxes, raised her eyebrows in surprise.

'What's all this lot, then? I didn't know we'd ordered anything.' She frowned and I knew she was thinking I'd done this without consulting her.

'We haven't,' I said shortly and handed her the card.

Her face cleared. 'From Bran? Oh, how wonderful! I didn't think he'd leave us in the soup without some kind of apology. But these are fantastic!' She bent and rummaged in the crates.

'What a lot of plants, too! And look, they're the same varieties that we were growing. He must have noticed — maybe he came down and had a peek when we weren't here. Jill, they'll more than make up for what we've lost!'

She looked at me as she straightened.

'What's up? You don't look very happy. Don't you realise that only two days ago we were staring ruin in the face?'

'Oh, um, nothing.' I pasted a smile on my face. 'I'm just stunned, that's all.' The expression 'coals of fire' had just crossed my mind.

Judy was still rattling on, consumed with excitement as she delved into the second box. 'Oh, isn't Bran kind? And how thoughtful of him to make it up to us in this way, rather than having to talk about money. What a nice guy he is.' She straightened up. 'I'll walk down to the shop in a minute. We're nearly out of milk. Can you think of anything else we need? I'll write a list if there is.'

'Not really,' I murmured, my mind elsewhere. 'I'll leave it you, okay? I'd better go up to the farm and thank Bran for these.' I stiffened my spine and reached for my jacket.

* * *

The door was opened by Marie, her expression a mask of polite enquiry. When she saw who it was, however, her eyes narrowed and all sign of politeness vanished. 'Oh, it's you.' She stood firmly in the doorway, blocking my entrance. 'What do you want?' she added with a glare.

'Good morning, Marie.' I looked her up and down. She was wearing an ankle-length flounced skirt of blue denim and a patterned jumper with a scoop neckline. Large hoop ear rings swung as she moved, and her hands glittered with rings.

'I want a word with Bran. Is he here or outside in the fields?' I stepped forward but she still barred my way.

'You can't come in and you can't see him.' She shook her head, and there was a look of triumph in her eyes as she added, 'He's ill.'

'*Ill?*' This was something I hadn't bargained on. 'What's the matter with him?'

'Who is it, Marie?' came a male voice

then, and as she whirled around I caught sight of Bran, in dressing gown and slippers, behind her. 'Oh, Jill, it's you. Come on through.' He turned a shoulder and beckoned me to follow him.

'I told her you were ill and she couldn't see you,' Marie put in as I pushed open the door, forcing her to stand back.

'Oh, rubbish. I'm not exactly bedridden.' As I followed in his wake down the passage Bran suddenly burst into a fit of coughing. 'Sorry,' he muttered, wiping a handkerchief across his face. 'In here.'

He led the way into his study, a room I'd not been in before. The farmhouse was a rambling old place with nooks and crannies everywhere. This was a typically male room adapted I thought, from some other use. A store-room maybe? There were a couple of leather armchairs, a computer and telephone on a desk in one corner, and bookcases filling one wall.

'Here, sit down.' He cleared a pile of farming magazines off one of the chairs and sank down onto the other. A fire was burning in the grate and the room was very warm, but Bran was looking pale and peaky — what my mother would have called 'whisht', the old Cornish word for out of sorts.

'What's the matter with you, Bran?' I asked. 'A cold, is it?'

He shook his head. 'No, nor flu either, and I'm not infectious so don't worry. It's just this damn cough. I get it now and again. Usually when I'm stressed. It's something I picked up when I was abroad.'

'It sounds pretty rough,' I remarked with concern, as he was seized by another outburst. 'Have you anything to take for it?'

'Oh yes, bottles and bottles of stuff, but it usually just has to run its course. I caught the draught from the door then as I left the room; that's what set it off now, although I had a headache all yesterday.'

He stretched out his legs to the fire and the leather mules he'd been wearing dropped from his feet. He was wearing the navy towelling robe I remembered from the night we'd met in the kitchen when I was staying here. This time I found myself wondering what, if anything, he had on underneath it. Certainly his legs were bare, as far up as I could see ... I dragged my thoughts away as Bran spoke and felt my colour rise. The room really was rather hot.

I cleared my throat and drew in a breath. 'Bran, I came to say a big thank-you for the plants,' I blurted. 'It was good of you. Especially after ... after I yelled at you so.'

Bran shrugged. 'Oh, that's okay. Water under the bridge and all that. If I recall, I snapped at you too.' He seemed distracted as he rubbed a finger over the deep cleft in his forehead. I thought of the problems he'd mentioned, but I dared not ask or offer sympathy, after the way he'd brushed me off before.

Bran turned red-rimmed eyes to mine. 'Were they all right? The plants, I mean.'

'Oh, yes. Fine. We've got a lot to do now, getting them in as soon as we can.'

The conversation was stilted and polite. As we both fell silent, I could sense things not said hovering in the air between us.

Then I jumped, startled as the door bumped open and Marie came bustling in with a glass of water and a bottle of tablets.

'Time for another couple of these,' she said soothingly, bending over Bran and placing a hand on his arm, shooting a sidelong glance at me as she did so. He swallowed the pills with a grunt and sighed as he leaned back onto the cushions.

I rose to leave. 'I won't stay, Bran. You're obviously not up to conversation.'

He lifted a hand. 'No, no, I'm all right, really,' he said wearily. 'It's just this damn cough.'

Marie took the glass from his hand and straightened. 'No, Bran, Jill's quite right; you'll only make it worse by talking.'

'I'll see you around, then,' I said as I shrugged on my jacket. 'Hope you feel better very soon.'

And I was the only one to see the triumphant gleam in Marie's eyes as she added, 'I'll see you out.'

* * *

Saturday afternoon came and went and Judy returned from the cinema with stars in her eyes and a broad smile spread across her face.

'You enjoyed it, then,' I said jokingly as her expression told its own story.

'Oh, yes, it was a brilliant film.' She did a little pirouette on one heel. 'You really should see it.'

'And good company too, I take it.'

She nodded happily. 'We looked around the shops afterwards, then we went for a coffee and Will started telling me about himself.' She slumped onto a chair and kicked off her shoes. 'Oh, that's better,' she sighed. 'Those heels were killing me.

'He's had enough of farm work, Jill. He only went up to Tregilly to work until his two younger sisters were through college. They're twins apparently.' She delved into her bag and pulled out a comb and mirror. 'His mother's a widow, you see, and she always relied on the wages Will brought in to help out with what she could earn from her own part-time job.' Judy ran the comb through her tangled curls. 'But now the girls are independent, she's found herself full-time work and Will feels he's free to lead his own life.' She pushed comb and mirror back into the bag and jumped to her feet, picking up her shoes in the other hand. 'His ambition is to be a motor mechanic. Remember when we bought the car, what a help he was?'

I nodded. 'Yes, I do.'

'Well, he's always been keen on

engines and would have loved to have had a proper career as an engineer. But he's willing to settle for working in a garage and perhaps one day setting up in business on his own account.' She turned back and leaned both elbows on the worktop, a seriousness replacing her former exuberance. 'Jill, he says he wants to move away from Cornwall in the near future. Where there are more opportunities, you know?' She pushed a strand of hair back from her forehead and anchored it behind her ear. 'And — ' Her eyes met mine and held. ' — he's more or less been offered a job up in Bedford if he wants to take it. Apparently he knows somebody there in the car industry.'

'So you're keen on him,' I replied, 'and afraid you'll lose him when he goes.'

Judy nodded dumbly and straightened. 'Yes,' she added quietly, leaving the room.

* * *

It took Judy and me a couple of days to plant up our new stock. We were so busy I hardly noticed that the sun was actually shining for once, and was even breathing a little gentle warmth into the muddy soil. I was only vaguely aware, too, that birds were singing in the hawthorn trees beside me, which were covered in new greenery, and that it was spring.

* * *

I was having a shower that evening when I heard the phone ringing and Judy's voice answering it. As she didn't call out to me I assumed it was personal and didn't hurry to go downstairs.

When I did so, she was just ringing off. She turned to me with a serious expression and spread her palms. 'That was Mum,' she said, and I could guess the rest. 'She's having the plaster taken off at the end of the week. Could I come up, as her neighbour is ill. She's not able to get to the hospital, and won't be able to manage, either, for a few days after she gets back.' Judy bit her lip and her shoulders slumped. 'I know it's only north Cornwall and not a million miles away, Jill, but I feel dreadful about deserting you again.'

My heart sank, but I put an arm around her and gave her a friendly squeeze. 'Don't be. At least we've got all those plants in. I can manage, so don't feel you have to hurry back. Stay as long as your mum needs you.'

'Oh — ' She gave me a weak smile and slowly shook her head. ' — at least it shouldn't be as long as it was last time. And her friend is just getting over flu, so she should be out and about before too long.' She glanced at her watch. 'But I must phone Will and tell him. We were going out again tomorrow evening.'

I felt my eyes widen. This affair was getting serious, then.

* * *

I drove Judy into Falmouth the following morning and saw her off at the station. Then I returned to an empty house, and a nursery garden full of work. I sighed and bent to my task of weeding between the rows of young shrubs. It was tedious but had to be done. I'd nearly finished when I heard a dog barking close at hand and looked up to see Bess bouncing around on the other side of the fence.

I rose, rubbing my stiff knees, and leaned over to stroke her soft coat. That was when I caught sight of Bran at the far side of the field, his back towards me, bent over a piece of machinery.

He must be feeling better. Good. I opened the gate and strolled towards him. 'Hi, Bran,' I said as he turned. 'It's good to see you out. Are you better?'

He rose and turned round with a smile, an oilcan poised in one hand, a dirty rag in the other. 'Hi, Jill. Yes, thanks.' He still wasn't looking too good, but I let it pass. Then I saw he was working on my battered rotavator that I'd abandoned in the ditch after the accident. I'd tried to get it working again but had given up until I could get some help. To see Bran quietly doing it for me gave me a little warm glow.

His gaze softened. 'Are the plants growing all right?' He lifted an eyebrow.

'Oh, yes, they're doing well. Look, it's really good of you to do this for me.' I indicated the machine. 'I couldn't manage to get it out of the ditch on my own, now that Judy's away.'

'Yes, Will told me she's gone up to her mother's.' He picked up the oilcan and squirted a drop into some crevice. 'This seems to be okay now.' He started up the engine and spoke over the roar. 'No major damage done, just a few scratches.'

'Oh, thanks ever so much.'

He switched off the engine. Into the silence that followed, I looked up and our eyes met and held. There was a softness in their depths that was having a most peculiar effect on my body. Then Bran said, 'You know, I do admire you and Judy for getting your business up and running like you've done. You've worked *so* hard.'

I felt my jaw drop in surprise. Praise was the last thing I'd expected. But coming from him it tasted very sweet.

'Well, th . . . thank you,' I stammered, and was about say more when we were interrupted by a shout from the top of the field. As I whirled round I saw Will waving frantically and calling Bran's name.

'Come on up here, Bran, quickly! You're needed urgently. Something's happened.'

13

I had been cut off in mid-sentence as Bran flung the oilcan and rag to the ground at Will's summons and was off over the field with the dog at his heels. Staring thunderstruck after him, I wondered what on earth was wrong. But I could hardly trail after him to find out. It was nothing to do with me; I would be seen as a nosy interfering busybody.

I was just washing up my tea-time dishes when I heard the sound of pounding feet. I glanced out of the window and was surprised to see Will, tousled hair flying in the wind, come running down the garden towards me. Alarmed by the look of urgency about him, I flung the door open as he came to a halt and paused for breath.

'Will! What's up?' I moved towards him and seized his arm.

'Oh, Jill, we're all in such a state up there.' He jerked a thumb towards the farm. 'It's young Ricky. He's just . . . disappeared!'

'Disappeared?' I stared blankly at Will for a moment as this news sank in. So this was what had happened! 'But . . . but . . . '

'I thought he might have come down here.' Will rasped a hand over his face. 'It's a long shot, I know, but we've searched everywhere else.'

'How long has he been missing?' I met his troubled gaze.

'It's been about an hour since we realised we hadn't seen him. We're at our wits' end up at the farm. We've searched all the outbuildings, called and called, set the dog onto it, but . . . nothing.' He spread his huge hands. 'Jill, do you mind if I take a look around your place?'

'Of course not. I'll come with you.' I hastily wiped my hands on the tea-towel. 'There's the greenhouse, the shed . . . Oh, he could have had an accident and be lying hurt somewhere.' My stomach lurched as the full implications hit me.

'I know. Bran's nearly out of his mind with worry. Ricky's never done anything like this before.'

While we strode around the garden and up through the nursery field, looking under every bush and tree, Will told me the whole story. 'It's Ricky's birthday today, you see, and they had a little party for him. Half a dozen or so of his classmates.' He paused and knelt down to peer underneath the shed. 'Bran thought it would be good for him to be able to show off the farm, and make him more popular at school, as all kids love animals, don't they?' He backed out and rubbed off his hands down his moleskin trousers.

We stopped to search the greenhouse, calling Ricky's name all the time, and even pulling out the empty trays and pots under the benches where he could not possibly be.

'Well,' Will continued the story as we

paced the ground together, 'after tea Marie suggested a game of hide-and-seek outside. They were getting a bit over-excited, you know, like kids do.' He half-turned to me and I nodded. 'She thought it would calm them down a bit before they went home.'

I drew away for a moment to look in the ditch where we had thrown the pile of cuttings from the privet hedge and turned them over. I straightened up with a sigh. There were so many places a small child could be hidden, both here and around the farm. It was like looking for the proverbial needle in a haystack. As Will and I went through the gate in our newly repaired fence and onto the farm land, he went on with the story.

'Well, all the other children were found and came back to the house, except Ricky. After they'd waited around for a while for him to show up, Bran told me, they began to worry. So they sent all the others home — the parents were turning up by then — and began to search in earnest.'

We reached the top gate and Will slid the bolt across to open it, carefully closing it behind us. 'When I left, Bran was seriously thinking of calling the police. But he was in a quandary, you see, not wanting to get them over here on a fool's errand if the boy's just having them all on. Maybe showing off in his way to his mates by refusing to be found.'

I felt my eyes widen as I stopped and stared at him. 'But Will, surely Bran can't take that chance, can he? Not when his son's life could be in danger.'

'Of course not.' Will shook his head. 'I'm sure he's reported it by now. And maybe Ricky's even turned up.'

'I only wish there was something I could do.' Biting my lip, I met Will's anxious eyes.

He nodded. 'Oh, Jill, so do I. But what else *can* we do? We've all hunted high and low, but we're really going to have to widen the search.' He frowned.

'That's when we'll need to bring the police in.'

I glanced up at him. 'Perhaps I'll come and have a look round the farm myself, shall I? A fresh eye on the scene, you know?' I hesitated. 'Or would Bran think I'm interfering?'

But my concern for Ricky was uppermost. I recalled the little boy's small, serious face the day he'd told me that he didn't have a 'proper' mummy, and my heart turned over.

I met Will's worried eyes. 'I feel I must do *something*, even if it's useless.'

Will shrugged his massive shoulders, his attention obviously somewhere else. 'OK, if you want to. Go ahead and look wherever you like. I'm going across to the house in case there's been any news.'

* ★ *

I wandered round to the back of the property where I'd never been before. Weaving my way through a group of

234

empty barns, I realised these must be the ones Bran had mentioned, that he wanted to develop. They certainly looked forlorn and neglected now. A couple of them were roofless and the slates that had come down were lying where they had fallen. Crows squawked from the rafters as I inspected each one. There was a smell of damp and decay and I only stayed long enough to make sure there was no sign of Ricky. I was actually glad that he *wasn't* here. The crumbling stone walls looked dangerously unstable, and it was no place to linger.

Walking on, I came to a smaller, low building divided into several sections, and leaned over the wall. A huge pink sow occupied this part, so big I thought she must be due to farrow soon. Lying comfortably stretched out on a pile of sweet-smelling straw, she opened one eye and took a look at me. Then seeing I was neither a threat nor a source of food, she gave a grunt and went back to sleep.

I was walking round behind the pigsty when I realised that the back of it was connected to another smaller annex by a hatch door. I'd seen this arrangement before, on other farms I'd visited as a child. It was where the newborn piglets could be kept away from the sow if necessary. They could be brought to her for feeding, but kept separate if there was any danger of her rolling on them. There was a mound of clean straw in here as well, ready for the litter when it was born.

I was just about to leave when I thought I saw a movement in the straw. Rats, was my first reaction. Ugh! I recoiled at the thought and took a step back, squinting against the fading light, warily watching for any further movement. I would have to tell Will if it *was* a rat, as it could be dangerous to small piglets.

But this was no rat. When another movement came, I could distinctly see a small white shoe, a trainer like most children wore these days. It was followed by another; then as the hump of straw fell away, Ricky emerged and slowly sat up, blinking and rubbing his eyes.

'Hello Jill,' he said and gave a huge yawn. 'Where's Marie?' He stood up and peered over the low wall. 'She was going to find me, not you.'

'Ricky, *everyone's* been out looking for you.' I stretched out a hand and pulled him out of the pen. 'They've all been very worried because they couldn't find you.'

I kept his hand in mine as we started to walk back, and with the other tried to pick the bits of straw out of his hair.

'But why are they worried?' The little boy looked up at me with a puzzled frown. 'Marie knew where I was.' He stopped, looking back and pointing to the pig sty. 'She found that place for me and said it was such a good one that my friends would never find me. She said I was sure to get the prize for the last person to be found, and I must stay there until she came for me.' Then his mouth turned down at the corners. 'But it was such a long time I got bored, and then I went to sleep.'

I squeezed Ricky's hand, puzzling over what he'd just said. I was equally as bewildered as he was.

I was rounding the corner of a barn with Ricky coming on behind, when I almost bumped into Marie coming the other way, with Bess the dog at her side.

'You!' She stopped dead in her tracks and her eyes narrowed. I jumped back, startled, as much from the poisonous look she darted at me as from her sudden appearance.

'Wh-what are *you* doing here?' she glared at me, frowning, one hand on her hip, the other on the corner of the wall. She was wearing bright pink narrow trousers and a fluffy jumper of lighter baby-pink that made her appear even more like a dainty porcelain doll. Except for the look on her face.

'The same as you, I imagine,' I replied coolly, staring her down.

Then, as Ricky came around the corner, Marie's expression changed in an instant as she gave all her attention to the child. As if it had been switched on, a beaming smile transformed her face, and I wondered if I'd imagined the whole thing.

'Oh, *Ricky*! You've found him! Thank goodness!' She bent down and clasped the child to her with both arms. 'Oh, my darling, at last!'

But the dog had run to Ricky and was excitedly jumping up and licking his face. He squirmed out of Marie's grasp, let go of my hand, and child and dog went running across the yard together.

'I want my prize!' the little boy called back over his shoulder. 'I'm going to find Dad.'

Before I could get a word in, Marie straightened up, and now the mask of dislike was back on her face.

'We've all been searching and searching — at our wits' end with worry over him — and all the time, he was with *you*!' She stabbed a finger at me. 'How dare you! You had him down at your place, didn't you? What have you been *doing* with him all this time? We thought he was lost — or worse. Bran's just called out the police!'

'Of course I didn't!' I felt my brows rise in astonishment at this attack. If it hadn't been so serious, I would even have laughed. 'Don't be so ridiculous, Marie. As if I'd take Ricky away without telling anyone! You must be out of your mind.'

'Well, if I am it's no wonder,' she snapped. 'We're all just about at breaking point with all this worry.' She turned on a heel, gave me a final glare and hurried after the child.

* * *

Well! If I hadn't heard Ricky's story from the child himself, I would have taken Marie's performance at face value, and believed her to be genuinely upset. But now I could see this was all an act that she was putting on purely for my benefit. She'd even had tears in her eyes.

Presumably it hadn't occurred to her that Ricky might have already told me what had happened, and her part in it. But I still couldn't fathom out *why* she should have wanted to cause such trouble. What were her motives? She must have had some reason for not wanting Ricky to be found.

Then suddenly as she flounced off after the child, everything clicked into place in my mind. This had all been carefully planned. As Ricky's voice echoed in my head, I began to see it all. 'Marie told me to hide . . . until *she* came back to find me . . . '

The deviousness of it! It was like some fantastic fairytale. I could hardly believe it. She had *plotted* Ricky's disappearance and cast herself in the role of the heroine who, when all else fails, finds the lost little boy and triumphantly restores him to his family. They are so grateful to her of course, and Bran most of all, that he realises at last how he could never manage without her, what a wonderful mother she would make for his son, and all ends happily ever after.

Wow! I had guessed from the beginning that Marie wanted Bran for herself, hadn't I? But who would imagine she would to go to such lengths! I wondered if she was mentally unstable, in which case I could feel sorry for her, or just desperate, when I wouldn't.

And now I, of course, having arrived at the wrong moment, had been cast in the role of the wicked witch who infiltrates the happy scene, comes between heroine and hero and thwarts her so-carefully laid plans. No wonder she had been less than pleased to see me.

⋆　⋆　⋆

I had been left reeling with astonishment as all this sank in, and now I turned back towards my own land, carefully sliding the bolt across the gate as I went through. I wanted no reappearance of those cattle on my land again.

Deep in thought, my eyes were on the ground, otherwise I would have missed it. But as I turned, I caught sight of something glittering in a ray of evening sunshine at my feet. I bent and picked up the tiny object, brushed the soil from it and examined it in the palm of my hand. Then I felt my eyes widen, and the sky turned turtle as realisation hit me like a slap in the face. It was a gilt-and-pearl drop earring.

And I knew exactly where I'd seen its twin. Marie again! My jaw dropped as this new revelation sank in. *She'd* unlocked that gate the other day! Deliberately. In order to cause havoc on my land and set me against Bran. I'd already thought her devious, but it had come to more than that. I realised now what a dangerous woman she was — a clever and ruthless one, and my sworn enemy.

My stomach churning, I carefully tucked the tell-tale bauble into a pocket and walked slowly down the field, wondering what I should do about this. Was I jumping to conclusions? On the face of things it *did* seem a far-fetched story, but I trusted my gut feelings. Instinct, intuition, whatever, it had never let me down yet.

But getting Bran to believe me was going to be much harder. Plus, said a small voice inside my head, what if he actually *was* keen on Marie? She was an attractive woman, after all. I could be totally wrong about the whole thing and about to make a fool of myself.

So what should I do? I could go to Bran right now and hand over the evidence. It would, however, sound like telling tales. So would the story behind Ricky's disappearance, if I told him that. Both would bring me down to Marie's level, and if there *was* anything going on between them, would lead only to huge embarrassment.

On the other hand, if Bran was, as I suspected, completely unaware, why *should* I keep quiet and let him walk blindly into the trap I was convinced Marie was setting up?

I stood biting my lip, trying to make up my mind as I stared unseeingly down the field to where the chimney of my cottage was poking up through the trees. Then I decided. If this was going to be open warfare between Marie and me, then it was a case of no-holds-barred.

I stiffened my spine, held my head high and strode on.

14

I decided to go up to the farm the very next day, before my courage failed me, and before Judy came back. It was all far too complicated, and too personal, to attempt explaining it to her.

It was a glorious morning of April sunshine. A few white puffball clouds were moving leisurely above my head in the azure blue of the sky, and from the hawthorn hedge as I passed came the rustlings and chirpings of birds busy at raising their families.

I fingered the tell-tale ear-bob in my pocket while my thoughts whirled. Having slept on the problem, it seemed now even less likely that Bran would believe what I was telling him. There was no way, of course, that I could prove where I'd found it, and my hunch that Marie lost it when she was tampering with the gate was just that

— guesswork. She would certainly say in her own defence that she could have dropped it anywhere.

I bit my lip and almost turned back home again. However, was I going to convince Bran I was telling the truth? Would he believe a woman's intuition? On the other hand, my defence was: why should I go to such lengths to make it up? I had nothing against Marie, or anything to lose.

Plus, there was Ricky's story. If I could get him to tell his father what he had told me, Bran might then be convinced. I sighed and gave a mental shrug.

Anyway, what was I getting so worked up about? The sun was shining, my plants were shooting up, Judy would soon be back and we could hopefully look forward to the customers who would soon come pouring in. So, why did I care so much about what was going on at the farm? I could just ignore Marie and her vindictiveness, say nothing at all about it, and get on with my own life. After all, what did any of it matter in the great general scheme of things?

But deep down I knew that it did.

★ ★ ★

So the following day I retraced my steps up to Tregilly and knocked on the door, steeling myself for another run-in with Marie. But it was opened instead by Mrs. Trelease.

'Oh, Jill my dear, hello, come in.' She widened the door and I stepped inside. 'How nice to see you. Has your garden recovered yet from the damage? I was so sorry to hear about all that.'

'Yes, thanks.' I smiled as we moved down the passage. 'Pretty much. And mostly because Bran replaced the plants for us so quickly.' I paused as she opened the sitting-room door and went to usher me in. 'Actually, I was wondering if I could have a word with him. Can you tell me where he is? Outside or in?'

'I think he's in his study, dear. Go and see.' She pointed down the passage. 'I haven't seen him come out.'

At that moment the study door opened and Bran emerged, his brows rising as he saw me.

'Jill, hello! I thought I heard your voice. Come on in.' He stood back and reentered the room. 'I was about to come down and see you as it happens,' he said, indicating a seat and perching himself on the swivel desk chair, with his back to the work he'd been doing. 'But I got bogged down in all this stuff.' He sighed and wearily pinched the bridge of his nose. He indicated the surface of the desk, piled high with what seemed to be computer print-outs of important-looking documents, the keyboard pushed askew to make room for them, as well as a pile of books on legal matters.

I remembered then. The day the cattle broke in, when I came up here and we had the row. Hadn't he muttered 'That makes two of us' when

I'd yelled at him that we were ruined? I knew he was short of money, of course; he'd told me that when he wanted to buy my land. But *ruined?* I looked at him in concern. I'd noticed how pale he was looking, and had put it down to the after-effects of his illness; but now I could see the worry-lines creasing his forehead.

Gently, I said, 'Bran, I don't want to pry, but you did tell me ages ago that you had money problems. Is it really bad?'

He gave a mirthless laugh. 'About as bad as it gets.' He stood up and restlessly paced the room. 'I'm so overdrawn the bank won't advance me any more money. I'm in debt to all these tradesmen.' He indicated the papers on his desk. 'And I'm pretty much on my beam ends here. Jill, I've got to face it — I'm going to have to put Tregilly on the market.' He slumped down into the chair again and leaned forward, hands on his knees and head bowed. He looked the picture of defeat, and my heart went out to him. I drew in a quick breath, instinctively reaching out to lay my hand on one of his.

'Oh, Bran, I'm so *sorry* it's come to this. And there is no other way?'

He shook his head, turned my hand over and squeezed it hard. I could feel the tension in his body as he struggled to control his emotions, before he placed his other hand over mine for a long moment and a small silence fell. Every bone in my body was melting at his warm grasp and longing for more.

Then the door suddenly burst open and Marie appeared with a steaming mug in her hand. 'Here's your coff . . . coffee, Bran.' Her voice faltered as her sharp eyes homed in on our clasped hands. 'Oh, I didn't know *you* were here,' she said, flashing me a look that would curdle milk. *Oh, no, not again*, I thought.

Bran let my hand drop and straightened up in his seat. 'Oh, thanks Marie,' he said curtly.

'I'll put it on the desk for you, shall

I?' Seeming in no hurry to leave, Marie hovered at his shoulder, brushing against him as she leaned over to reach behind.

'No,' Bran snapped, 'there's not room there. Give it to me.' He stretched out a hand, but not before I'd seen her openly staring at the papers on his desk.

Taking the coffee from her, he turned towards me. 'Would you like one as well, Jill?'

'Oh, no, no thanks.' Shaking my head, I almost smiled as I imagined what Marie's reaction would be if I'd accepted.

'Oh, I forgot the biscuits,' Marie said, laying a hand on Bran's arm and looking up into his face as she edged past him. 'We've got some of those chocolate ones. You know, your favourites. I'll go and get them.'

'No, forget it. I don't want any biscuits.' Bran shook his head, then must have realised how abrupt he sounded. 'Thanks.'

Having no reason to stay any longer, Marie backed slowly out of the room, pointedly leaving the door open.

I rose and closed it behind her. 'Do you think she heard what you were saying?' I said to Bran.

He shrugged. 'Maybe. But who cares? I shall have to tell my parents soon, anyway. And I'm certainly not looking forward to that.' Wearily, he rubbed a hand over his face and sighed. 'Anyway, let's change the subject.' He straightened his shoulders and sat back. 'I'm forgetting to say why I was on the way down to see you. Jill, I can't *begin* to thank you for finding Ricky for us last night,' he said earnestly, as our eyes met.

'Oh, no, that's okay,' I said. 'I'm only too glad I was there at the right moment, when he woke up and moved, otherwise I would have walked straight past him.'

'I'm still a bit mixed up about what actually happened though.' Bran slowly shook his head and frowned.

'Ricky tells me it was you who found him. Although apparently Marie had told him to stay there until *she* did.' He spread his hands. 'And what I can't understand is, if she knew where he was all the time, why she left it until we were so worried before going to fetch him.' Still looking perplexed, he stared into the distance for a moment.

'Anyway, Jill — ' His gaze swivelled back to me. ' — thanks again. As I said, we were desperate by that time. I actually had the phone in my hand, about to call the police, when Ricky turned up shouting for his prize!' He smiled and ran a hand through his hair. Then the smile vanished and he frowned again. 'But as I said, I can't seem to get a straight answer out of Marie.'

My stomach lurched. This was the moment. The golden opportunity and the opening I'd been hoping for. Nervously I cleared my throat. It was now or never. Bran was obviously puzzled — maybe he *would* believe me. Anyway, there would never be a better time. I broke the eye contact, swallowed hard and plunged in.

'Er, Bran . . . about Maric.' I hesitated, twisting my hands in my lap.

'Mm. What about her?'

'Well, you may or may not have noticed she's always very cool towards me.'

'Oh, I can't say I have, particularly.' Bran crossed one leg over the other and gave me his full attention.

'Do you remember when I was staying here and we met in the night, how she spied on us and jumped to the wrong conclusion?'

Bran's face lifted with a hint of amusement. 'Oh . . . yes. Yes, I do, now you mention it.'

'Well, ever since then she's been very unpleasant to me.' I hastily shook my head. 'Oh, I'm not complaining — don't think that,' I added before he could get the wrong impression. 'I couldn't care less. But I think I know why, and as it concerns you, I think you should be told.'

'Me?' I'd obviously captured Bran's interest now, as he folded his arms and gave me his full attention. 'Did you say it concerns *me?*' He fixed wide eyes on my face.

I nodded. 'Bran, she sees me as a rival.'

He looked blankly back at me. 'A rival for what?'

'For your affections!' When his expression didn't change, I stabbed a finger at him in exasperation. 'Men! Oh, Bran, how can you live in the same house and not realise? Marie wants to be . . . well, more than an employee,' I said slowly and clearly, spelling it out to him. 'Don't you understand yet? Haven't you noticed how indispensable she tries to make herself? How she's made your mother reliant on her, how she seems to dote on Ricky as if he was *her own child?*' I paused for breath. '*Now* do you see what I mean?'

'You're joking!' Bran's jaw dropped

and a look of pure astonishment spread across his face. 'But . . . but . . . I've never . . . '

'No, you haven't. But she wants you to.' I smiled at his complete bafflement. 'So much so that she organised that game of hide-and-seek to give herself an opportunity to play the heroine.' I paused for breath. 'She thought that finding Ricky when no one else could was a way of getting in with you. He's telling you the truth, Bran,' I said, nodding. 'Marie told him to stay there and not move until *she* found him. Ricky told me so himself.' I let this sink in before I went on. 'Then I came along and spoilt it all. No wonder she wouldn't even give me the time of day when she let me in the other morning.'

'Jill, are you sure about all this? Bran's forehead wrinkled. 'It seems very farfetched to me.'

'It does. But I am sure. Because . . . that's not all.'

'Not *all?* Isn't that enough? Whatever else can there be?' He raised his hands in bewilderment.

'This.' I reached into my pocket and drew out the earring. Bran stared at it, totally perplexed, a frown furrowing his forehead.

'Now look, I'm not out to cause trouble for Marie,' I said firmly. 'Let's make that clear. But I really do think you ought to know about this. Because it belongs to Marie. I've seen her several times wearing the pair.' I drew in a breath. 'Now, I found this one dropped on the ground beside the gate between your field and mine, *where the cattle came through*.' I paused to let Bran take this in. 'Did you ever solve the mystery of why the gate was open that time?'

He shook his head. 'Jill, I've thought and thought about it. I closed it myself that night, I know I did. I remember particularly because Bess was dancing around my feet, getting in the way, and I had to hold her back so I could fasten the padlock.'

'I suppose you asked the rest of the

family if they went out after you, and maybe forgot to close it?'

'Yes, of course I did!' he snapped and immediately apologised. 'Sorry, Jill. But yes. It was almost dark when I came in, and Mum and Dad wouldn't have ventured out after that.'

'Did you ask Marie?'

'Um, no. As a matter of fact, I couldn't find her. She wasn't around at the time. But she never has anything to do with the outside. She's no reason to; she's only paid to keep house and help Mum look after Ricky.'

'So, maybe this solves the mystery.' I held up the trinket. 'Although I can't prove it. But in view of what I've already told you, what do you think?

Bran frowned. 'Well, it's a lot to take in, I admit, but I suppose you could be right. It all seems to fit.'

I let out a long sigh of relief. At least he hadn't dismissed the whole thing out of hand.

'But I've never looked at Marie in that way.' He stared at me and slowly shook his head. 'Or even thought about it. It just wouldn't occur to me. She's very good at what she does, and I've probably told her so at odd times. I did help her once, to sort out some problem with her finances, and she was very grateful, but that's as far as it goes. Fancy her thinking . . . ' Bran spread his hands and slowly shook his head. 'Jill, I don't know what to do now.'

'You needn't do anything,' I replied firmly. 'Just be aware, that's all. Marie *wants* you to notice how good she is at the job. I told you, she's getting at you through your mother, and through Ricky.'

Bran nodded absently, gazing into the fire, and rasped a hand across his jaw.

So there wasn't anything between them after all. I'd got my answer to that and I felt my heart give a little lift, and not entirely because I'd been saved from embarrassment. I relaxed and pressed home my point. 'Plus, all that make-up and jewellery she wears is meant to attract *your* attention, you know. Bran, I'm not being catty, honestly.' I spread my palms. 'But have you ever seen a home-help dress like she does?'

Then as he raised his head, I realised again how tired he was looking. It was time for me to go. I'd said what I'd come to say; now he could digest it all.

I moved to get up. 'Anyway, I'll leave you alone now, and let you get on with your work.' I rose and picked up my jacket. 'And . . . ' I hesitated. ' . . . I really hope you can find some way around your problems.'

He gave me a weary smile. 'Thanks, Jill,' he said, meeting my eyes, 'and thanks too for coming and telling me all this. You've certainly given me plenty to think about.'

'I'm sorry to have piled more trouble on your plate. But at least now you're aware of what's going on, you'll recognise what Marie's up to. Bye now.'

I'd been standing with my hand on the handle of the door as I spoke, and when I opened it I caught a glimpse of Marie stepping quickly back into the kitchen, which was right next to the study. It was obvious she'd been eavesdropping. However, not a bit shamefaced at being caught out, she stood her ground in the doorway and glared at me. 'I know what you're up to. I heard every word,' she hissed in a low voice, pulling the door partway across. In the background I could see Mrs. Trelease on the other side of the room talking and laughing with Ricky.

'Making up stories about me. Worming your way in here. Trying to drive a wedge between Bran and me.' The pretty doll-face was contorted with spite. 'It won't work, you know. He depends on me too much for you to get a look-in.' She stuck her chin in the air, sniffed and tossed her hair back.

'Oh, Marie, don't be so childish. Haven't you heard that eavesdroppers never hear good of themselves? I've told you before you've no reason to feel jealous of *me*.' I sighed and turned to leave.

But I could see, over Marie's shoulder, that while Ricky was still sitting at the table absorbed in some game, Bran's mother had now crossed the room to the doorway and was standing right behind her. She must have heard everything Marie had said.

I raised my hand in farewell to her and smiled to myself as I saw Marie whirl round and the two women come face-to-face.

Then I slipped quietly out of the house.

★　★　★

Will was in the field as I went down it on the way home, and I could see he was checking the job on the rotavator that Bran had abruptly left when Ricky had gone missing. He had begun to guide it down the field, and now gave a wave as he saw me coming.

'I was just taking this down to your

place,' he said as we met. 'Bran told me he'd got it working okay again, and that it's only a bit dented and scratched. You'll be able to use it whenever you like.'

'Oh, Will, that's really good of you — and Bran.' I laid a hand on the machine and helped him push it down the field. 'Thanks. But after what happened last time, I shall think twice about using it on my own again.'

'Good idea.' We walked on a few paces. 'So Judy's coming back on Friday, then,' he said as we stopped to open the gate.

I stared at him in amazement as I felt my brows rise. '*Is* she? Well, she hasn't told me anything about it. How do you know?'

I felt a stab of annoyance that Judy should have told Will this news before me, then told myself not to be so childish. If as it seemed, these two *were* becoming a couple, it was only natural.

I'd had a couple of calls from Judy

keeping me in touch with developments, but not for a few days now.

'Oh, I had a text from her yesterday.' I noticed Will's colour heighten as he spoke. 'I've heard from her a few times since she went.' He turned to me as we manhandled the machine into the shed. 'I'm sure you'll have a message from her soon. I said I'd pick her up from the station actually. I've got to go into Falmouth anyway on Friday.'

'Oh, I see.' So it seemed they *were* rapidly becoming a twosome. What next, I wondered.

15

Judy arrived back as arranged, the following Friday, full of apologies for being away for so long.

'Anyway, Mum's fine now, so I shouldn't have to go up there anymore.' Judy flung down her bag and leaned her elbows on the worktop. 'She's got her confidence back now, and seems to have made a close friend in this neighbour. I think they prop each other up.' She smiled and hooked a lock of curly hair behind one ear. 'It's a huge relief for me.'

'It's good to see you.' I smiled back, regarding Judy closely. She was looking really well. Carefully made up, her eyes were shining, and she was dressed more smartly than usual, in a narrow ankle-length brown skirt with a jumper of soft emerald and new boots. 'A lot's happened since you've been away.'

'Yes, so Will was saying.' She cut me short, twirled on a heel and reached for the kettle. 'Drink?'

'OK, coffee please. I've got a chicken casscrole in the oven for later.'

'Lovely. I thought I could smell something yummy.' She joined me on the sofa in the window alcove as we chattered away, catching up. 'How's business?' she asked eventually, upending her mug.

'Not that great, to be honest.' I shrugged. 'Ticking over, but no huge profits coming in as yet.'

'Oh.' Judy's face fell. 'Well, tomorrow I'll get stuck in and do my share. Right now though, I must unpack and freshen up.' She rose and carried her empty mug to the sink. With her back to me she added casually, 'Will's picking me up later. We're going out for a drink.' She turned her head and looked at me over her shoulder. 'Er, do you fancy coming too?'

I shook my head. No way was I going to play gooseberry to those two.

'Thanks, but no thanks.' I smiled. 'I've got a few phone calls to make. I haven't spoken to *my* mum in ages.'

★ ★ ★

A few days passed, during which I was becoming increasingly concerned about Judy. Since arriving back she'd seemed very preoccupied and not her usual bouncy self. She worked as hard I did, but there were long periods when she seemed to be lost in her own thoughts, sometimes not even hearing me when I spoke to her. After a couple of days of this I'd had enough, so I confronted her one evening after dinner when we were clearing away.

'Judy, you didn't hear a word of what I just said, did you?' I challenged her as I flung a handful of cutlery into a drawer and slammed it shut. 'Is there something wrong?' I took a step closer to her and looked into her face. 'You're not ill or anything, are you?'

To my surprise she threw both arms

around my neck and there were tears in her eyes when she drew back, shaking her head. 'No, no, nothing like that. But . . . oh Jill, I'm sorry. I've been thinking and wondering for ages how best to break this to you.'

I could guess what was coming and was half-prepared as she went on. 'You know I told you about Will and his new job?' I nodded. 'Well, he has to go up there next week if he's taking it at all. Of course it's a once-in-a-lifetime opportunity, and . . . '

' . . . you've decided to go with him,' I finished for her.

Judy nodded dumbly. The tears were welling up again as she threw open her hands. 'Oh, Jill! I feel so *bad* about leaving you, but I know I must. I love Will so much, you see. It would just break my heart to leave him.'

'Of course I understand.' I patted her shoulder consolingly. 'You mustn't feel bad. This was always on the cards. We knew that from the beginning. It was part of our agreement, remember? And it could equally well have happened to me.'

If only. But the conversation had turned to practical matters. There was a great deal to talk about.

★ ★ ★

Judy and Will left Cornwall together at the weekend, after an emotional parting between us.

'I'll send for the rest of my stuff after we're settled,' she said, heaving a loaded hold-all down the stairs to add to the pile by the gate. Over the wall that divided Lizzie Pascoe's cottage from the Taylors' I caught a glimpse of Will's tall figure doing the same.

At that moment the taxi drew up outside and as Judy turned to me for one last hug, we both had tears in our eyes.

'Oh, Jill, this is it.' Judy's mouth trembled. 'Goodbye, all the good luck in the world with the business, and I'll phone you as soon as I possibly can.'

I nodded and sniffed as I whispered in her ear, 'You too. And Ju, I wish you both all the happiness there is. You've got a good man in Will, and he's found himself a treasure in you.'

I drew back, as with a wobbly smile she swung her shoulder bag over her arm, joined Will in the taxi and they roared off into their future together.

* * *

Later that day, I heard a knock at the door and opened it to find Bran standing on the step. 'Hi, Jill. Can I come in for a minute?'

'Oh . . . Bran! . . . Hello. Of course.' To my annoyance, I felt my heart rate starting to speed up as usual at his unexpected appearance, as I stood back for him to enter.

He was wearing a moss-green sweater over fawn chinos, and as he dipped his head in the low doorway and came through, I could see he had a beaming smile on his face, his eyes were shining and there was a general air of suppressed excitement about him.

Not knowing quite what to say, I seized on the banal. 'You're looking much better,' I said formally. 'Are you over that awful cough at last?' At the moment he was looking on top of the world. In fact I'd never seen him in such a buoyant mood.

'Yes, yes, absolutely.' He brushed this aside with a dismissive wave of his hand. 'Jill, I've had such a piece of good news, I just had to come and tell you,' he gabbled. 'You'll never believe it. I can hardly believe it myself!'

Then to my amazement he threw both arms around me, lifted my feet off the floor and twirled me round. I gasped as walls and ceiling seemed to change places, before at last he set me down again. I squealed and laughed, grasping his arm to steady myself as the room still rocked. But rather than let me go as I moved to step away, Bran kept both hands on my shoulders, and we looked steadily into each others' eyes.

There was a long moment of closeness as neither of us moved. And as the crackle of tension in the air increased, my treacherous body began sending out signals I found hard to control. My heart was thumping so loudly against Bran's chest, I was sure he must be aware of it. I held my breath, waiting for what must surely come.

For at long last I had to be honest with myself. I'd fallen in love with this man. Totally and completely. It hadn't been something I'd expected, or wanted to happen. Until I'd met Brandon Trelease I'd prided myself on being in control of my life, happily independent, running my own business and answerable to no one. However, I hadn't bargained for this. I was the one now being controlled. Helpless against the sheer force of this man's charisma, I was being pulled towards him as relentlessly as the tides by the moon. For months he'd always been at the back of my mind, all through every day, while by night his ghost stalked my dreams.

Motionless in Bran's arms, the moment lengthened. Then he gave me a squeeze, dropped a brief peck on my cheek, and drew away. I staggered with weakened knees to the sofa and fell into it. Anti-climax hit me like a slap in the face and left me speechless. Every nerve in my body was left so on edge with frustration I almost screamed.

Totally unaware of all this, of course, Bran folded himself into the small space beside me, crossed his long legs and sat down. 'Jill, as I said, I just had to come and tell you. Mum and Dad are pleased of course, but they don't really understand the importance of it. And I know you will.'

His expressive eyes met mine. They were dancing with excitement, yet with a tenderness in their depths that did nothing for my composure. So, obviously he didn't feel the same way about me. Well, it was something I would have to live with, and not betray by word or gesture that we were anything but good friends and neighbours. It would be hard, but I could face it. Better this way than if Bran should guess my feelings and laugh at the very idea, as he had done when I told him about Marie spying on us in the night. I'd never really forgotten how much that had hurt. So I pasted a bright smile on my face and half-turned towards him.

'Well, come on, what *is* it?' I said briskly, shifting slightly away from the unnerving warmth of his shoulder against mine, and trying not to make it too obvious. 'I'm dying to know.'

Bran smiled and turned lively eyes to me. 'Jill, do you remember I told you about that piece of land down by the creek that belongs to me, but I can't do anything with?'

'Mm. Yes.' I nodded and waited for him to go on.

'And the old relics of the mining industry that are down there?' Not waiting for a response, he flung out both hands as his face lit up. 'Jill — I've sold it!'

'*Sold* it? You *have?*' Genuinely surprised, I felt my brows rise, then crease in a frown of bewilderment. 'B . . . but who would want it if it's useless?'

'That's what's so amazing.' Bran wriggled in his seat, too excited to stay still. 'There's apparently been a conservation group set up to salvage and restore what's left of the ancient relics, before they vanish forever.'

'Really?' I felt my eyes widen. Now I was beginning to see why he was so jubilant.

'And the quay.' He turned briefly. 'I told you about the quay, didn't I?'

'Yes.' I nodded. 'You did. Go on.'

'Well, they say it's important for that to be preserved. So, Jill, they've offered me a really good price for it! For the quay itself, plus the piece of land around it, where there are some bits and pieces of old rusting machinery.' He clasped his hands together in delight, then widened them and shrugged his shoulders. 'Good luck to them, I say. They're welcome to whatever they want. I shall be so *glad* to get rid of it.' He shifted position again and crossed the other leg.

'But that's wonderful!' The smile on my face was a reflection of his own. 'Oh, Bran, I'm *really* pleased for you.'

'Thank you.' He gave me another beaming grin. 'It solves all my problems, you see. The money will finance my plans for the barns, plus the group are going to put in a road to get to the quay, which will be perfect for my access too. It's *all* perfect.' He gave a huge sigh. 'I would never have believed it a few days ago. You remember how I was within an inch of putting the farm on the market? Now I shall be able to move on with the developments. At last!'

'Oh, Bran, I really am delighted for you.' Then I paused and looked down at my folded hands. 'And for myself as well, in a way. Because you know, I've always felt so guilty about not letting you run that road through my land.' I raised a hand as he tried to protest. 'I know you said forget it, but I couldn't. I've had it on my conscience ever since.' I lifted my head and smiled. 'So now we're both happy.'

'Well, 'happy' doesn't half describe it.' Bran grinned. 'I'm absolutely over the moon, as you can imagine.' Restless, he uncrossed his legs again, rose to his feet and paced the room. 'Tell you what, Jill. Why don't we take a walk down there?' Stuffing his hands in his pockets, he looked down at me, rocking on his heels, his head almost reaching the ceiling beams. 'I could show you exactly what they're going to do, if you're interested. I'm so worked up I can't settle anyway. I need to talk to someone. Would you like to?'

'Of course I would,' I said with enthusiasm. Being left alone to run the business and seeing Judy so happy with Will had left me not envious exactly, but disturbed. This would take my mind off my own problems for a while.

* * *

We strolled down through the woods towards the creek. On each side of the path the great beech trees were a haze of bright new foliage, and beneath them danced sheets of bluebells, filling the air with their faint sweet perfume.

Beside the track, a little stream of clear water ran chuckling to itself over a bed of shining pebbles, on its way to join the river and ultimately, the sea. Not for nothing was this way called Lovers' Lane. It was a place just made for romance. I glanced up at the tall figure striding beside me and thought wistfully how different things might have been.

'Here we are,' Bran said as we went down a flight of steps onto the strip of shingle beside the river. Pebbles and seashells crunched beneath our feet as we avoided the twists of mooring ropes that spread across our path. Stunted trees, defying all the laws of gravity, clung to the bank beside us, their twisted roots like clawing hands, while from their branches the blown shreds of dry weed fluttered in the breeze like exotic flowers.

'Ricky loves it down here,' Bran remarked. 'He and the dog would spend all day splashing about in the water if they could. It's a pity I don't have as much time to spend with him as I'd like. And Marie doesn't like getting her shoes muddy.'

We had come now to a great fallen tree, its branches reaching into the water; and rather than climb over it, we both had the same idea and perched on its smooth, weatherworn trunk, still warm from the day's sunshine.

I smiled, looking out over the sparkling water. 'He's a nice little kid, Ricky. You must be very proud of him.' I glanced towards Bran. 'He's a credit to all of you for the way he's been brought up.'

Bran turned and gave me a long look. 'I thought you didn't like children, Jill. When you said that time you couldn't stand teaching.'

'Oh, but those kids were stroppy teenagers,' I protested. 'I really like younger ones. I think I made a mistake in my career actually. I should have gone in for juniors instead. They're easier to deal with, so I'm told. More interested in learning, too.' I wriggled into a more comfortable position and raked my unruly hair out of my eyes. The breeze was freshening and blowing it all over the place.

Bran nodded. 'Oh. Oh, I see,' he said and fell silent as if he was deep in thought. 'Anyway,' he said at last, brightening, 'that's my plot just over there.' He pointed to a small promon-tory on the other side of the tree trunk where we were sitting. 'See that grass-covered square wall with the little wood behind it?' I narrowed my eyes and followed his finger, then nodded. 'That's the quay. And down the bank a bit are the pieces of rusty old machinery I was telling you about, that were once part of the mining process.'

'Oh, right. I see what you mean.' I peered downstream and understood. 'And the road, I suppose, would run from there up behind those houses at the top of the hill, would it?'

'Yes. And straight back to the main road, where I can get access to Tregilly and avoid that awful corner altogether.' Bran's face was wreathed in smiles.

'Wonderful,' I replied as he rose to his feet and stretched out a hand to help me down.

Then, disturbingly, he kept the hand tucked into his own as we climbed the steps and strolled all the way back.

* * *

It hadn't meant a thing, I told myself later. Of course it hadn't. A casual gesture, born of the general euphoric mood Bran had been in, that was all. But I couldn't forget the feeling of his firm, strong hand in mine, and knew I wanted more than that from him.

He'd also dropped another quick kiss on my cheek as we'd parted, the kind one would give an old friend, or a child. And I was neither.

* * *

The feeling of loss was still with me next day as I went back outside to work, my head full of what might have been. *For goodness sake, take your mind off Brandon Trelease,* I told myself sternly, wrestling with a patch of dandelions outside the cottage window. *You can't let him take over your life. He's just not interested, else he would have made some sign long before now. He's had opportunities enough. So get a grip and forget the whole idea.*

But thinking over my present problems brought Bran to my mind even more. With the huge stroke of luck he'd had, he could well afford to employ other help to replace Will. But I couldn't. In spite of the reassurances I'd given Judy, I was now in a hole. So deep I didn't see how I was going to drag myself out of it.

If *only* I could sell my house. But it wouldn't happen because I wanted it to. It had been on the market for so long. The last thing I needed was to lower the asking price. Maybe I should change agents . . . although that would cost something, I supposed. My thoughts drifted round and round in circles, getting nowhere.

16

'How're you managing without Judy, then?' I jumped as Lizzie Pascoe's tightly permed head appeared over the hedge. 'I should think you're missing her some lot.'

'Oh, hello, Lizzie.' I stood up and rubbed the small of my back, stiff from kneeling. 'Yes, I certainly am. But I'm glad she and Will are so happy.'

Lizzie nodded. 'Heard from them, have you?' She settled herself more comfortably and leaned her arms on the wall, obviously prepared for a chat. I had a thousand things to do but couldn't bring myself to cut her off in mid-flow.

'Oh, yes,' I said with a smile, 'she's phoned several times and I had a long letter from her yesterday. She's so worried about leaving me, she keeps on apologising, although I've told her over and over not to feel guilty.'

'You won't never cope with this great place on your own, though, will you?' The woman echoed my own thoughts as she raised a hand that took in both the cottage garden and the two fields beyond. 'Going to employ someone to give you a hand, are you?'

'Can't afford to, Lizzie,' I replied abruptly.

'Aw.' She fell silent for a moment. A robin appeared out of nowhere and perched on a bush close beside me, cocking its head and chirping as if it had come to join in the conversation.

'Business idden too good, then, is it?' Lizzie's beady little eyes gazed into mine as her brows lifted.

I shook my head, at last admitting out loud what I'd known myself for a while, but had shied away from facing. 'It could be better, Lizzie. We had a good period over Easter, but since then it seems to have tailed off.'

'Ah.' She nodded sagely and pursed her lips. 'You do need help, my handsome. Men's help. 'Tis hard work, this here. Too hard for a maid on her own.' She tapped her fingers on the top of the wall. 'I'll tell you what you could do, though.' She paused as I parted the branches of a bush growing by the wall, and edged a little closer.

I raised an eyebrow in interest. 'Mm? What's that, then?'

'I was just thinking. When old Ed Jolly down to Penryn was turning his field into that there wildlife place, he had some of they students up to the college in to help him.' Her brow furrowed in further thought. 'Volunteers, they was, learning horticulture, see, and they did it for the experience, like. Put in dozens of trees, they did. Dug ponds and planted all sorts. Do that, could you?'

'Students?' I felt my eyes widen. 'Volunteers? Oh, I don't know, Lizzie.' I bit my lip and frowned. 'It sounds a wonderful idea, but I'd have to think about it.' However, my spirits had lifted at the thought of help of any kind that wasn't going to cost money. 'There must be rules and regulations of some kind, I suppose. I'd have to look into all that first.'

'Tell you what.' Lizzie unfolded her arms and straightened. 'You know Annie Bryant and her husband who do keep the shop?'

'Of course I do; they've taken my flowers several times. What about them?'

'Well, their boy Tom is up the college. I was wondering if he'd be interested. Ask them for you, shall I?' she said eagerly. 'I'm just going down there now.'

Inwardly smiling at her keenness to be involved, I nodded. 'That would be lovely. You could just ask him to call round for a chat if he likes the idea, and we can go through it all together. And thanks, Lizzie,' I called after her, as with a wave of her hand she disappeared behind the wall. I went back to work and smiled again as, a few minutes later, I saw her dumpy little figure trotting importantly down the road towards the village.

Later that evening I answered the doorbell to find a tall and gangly dark-haired youth on the doorstep, accompanied by a shorter, stocky one with a mane of flaming ginger. 'Hello, I'm Tom Bryant.' The tall one extended a hand, adding unnecessarily, 'and this is Ginger.'

'Come in,' I said with a smile. 'It's nice to see you. Have a seat. Tea? Coffee?'

Soon we were sitting around chatting like old friends. They were nice lads whom I instinctively felt I could trust. 'Well, come and have a look around outside, if you've finished your drinks, and I'll show you what there is to be done.'

The comments they made as we toured the garden centre convinced me they were both genuinely interested and also reasonably knowledgeable about plants and the work involved. And by the time they were ready to leave I was sure this was the answer to my problems, and we'd agreed they should come at weekends and part of the college holidays for as long as I wanted them.

'So I'll provide you with lunch and as much tea and coffee as you can drink. Okay?' I said with a smile as they were leaving. 'And I won't crack the whip *too* hard, I promise!'

As they both burst out laughing, I closed the gate behind them with a final 'See you on Saturday' and a wave as they went round the corner and out of sight.

★   ★   ★

Tom and Ginger turned up regularly during the following weeks, proving themselves to be reliable and trustworthy workers. They were perfectly capable of working on their own or together, at whatever task I set them, and were such an immense help that I blessed the day Lizzie had suggested the idea.

One evening when I was clearing up after my solitary meal, I picked up the phone when it rang and found it was Judy on the line. There was such a feeling of contained excitement in her voice as we went through the preliminary 'How are you's and so on, that I felt sure she must be leading up to something.

'Will's been taken on permanently and absolutely loves the job. We've found a lovely little flat overlooking the park, and Jill . . . you'll never believe this.' She paused and drew breath. 'He's asked me to marry him! We're actually engaged!'

I felt my brows shoot up to my hairline at this news and opened my mouth to reply, but Judy had gone rattling on and there was no way I could get a word in.

'He popped the question last night and I wanted you to be one of the first to know.' Laughing and sobbing at the same time, Judy's voice echoed down the line in a flurry of emotions and at last came to a halt.

'Oh, *Ju*,' I squealed, my voice rising up the scale, 'I am so *thrilled* for you! That's absolutely wonderful news. Many, many congratulations to you both. I know you'll be happy together — you're just made for each other.'

'Thank you,' she said simply. 'I'm so excited I don't know if I'm coming or going. But I know we're doing the right thing.'

'Well, give Will a hug from me with my very best wishes. Have you made any plans for the wedding yet? When's that going to be?'

And we spent the best part of an hour on the line discussing the endless arrangements to be made for the most important day of Judy's life.

★　★　★

Next morning I was in the potting shed, tidying up an accumulation of clutter that had mounted up over the weeks when I'd been on my own with no time to sort it. Now that the pressure had lifted a little, I could catch up on small jobs like this.

'I see you've got some help in, then.'

I jumped like a frightened rabbit and whirled around as the familiar voice came out of nowhere and Bran's tall figure appeared at the open door.

I straightened up and wiped my dirty hands down my jeans as I came up from the far end to meet him. 'Oh, hello, Bran.' I hooked my flyaway hair behind my ears and smiled as my heart started thudding in the usual infuriating fashion. 'Yes. They're students from the horticultural college. Volunteers, helping me out of a hole and gaining practical experience for themselves too.'

'Very neat. I thought that must be it when I recognised the Bryant boy. All right, are they?'

'Brilliant,' I replied with enthusiasm, suppressing a grin as his appearance reminded me of Lizzie Pascoe's need to know everything that was going on. 'I couldn't have coped without them after

Judy left. Now I'm getting a bit more on top of things.' I propped a shoulder on the doorframe. 'How are you managing without Will? Have you replaced him yet?'

'Yes, I have, actually.' Bran placed a booted foot on an upturned bucket and leaned on his knee. 'He's a chap from Penryn who's been out of work for a while. He seems okay; he's certainly a hard worker. We get on all right, but I do miss Will, after all the years he was with me.' He half-turned. 'He seems very happy and settled in the new job. I had a postcard from him the other day.'

'The other day? So you haven't heard the news, then?'

'News?' Bran arched an eyebrow. 'No, what news?'

'Will and Judy are getting married! I just heard from her. Isn't it great?'

He gave a low whistle and a smile spread across his face. 'Wow, are they really? Wonderful! They're very well suited, aren't they?'

I nodded, my attention distracted by

Tom, who was hurrying down the hill towards us. The sense of urgency about him made me wonder if there was something wrong.

'I came to tell you some news as well,' Bran said.

I jerked back to him and what he was saying. 'Oh? What's that then?'

'Mum and I between us decided to dismiss Marie.'

'*Dismiss* her?' I gasped, as guilt instantly homed in. 'Oh, Bran! Because of what I said? But I told you I didn't want to make trouble for her . . . '

'No, no, don't blame yourself at all. That had nothing to do with it,' he said firmly. 'Mum overheard what Marie was saying to you as you went out, and it confirmed what she'd been suspecting all along. It was the final straw, a kind of catalyst really. So we gave her a generous pay-off in lieu of notice and she's gone.'

'Oh, my goodness. Bran, how will you manage without her?'

'It's all settled. Mum's engaged a

woman she knows who lives in the village, to come in daily. She's got a son of Ricky's age — they go to school together — and she's quite happy to take them both to and fro. Now he's growing up, he doesn't need the same care as he did when he was a baby and a toddler. There's no need for anyone to live in.'

'That's wonderful. I hope it all works out for you. Oh . . . Tom.' I turned as the boy came up to us. Now I could see that he was carrying a tray of young bedding plants in each hand and that there was a general air of excitement about him.

'Hey Jill, take a look at these,' he said, then nodded towards Bran. 'Hi, Mr. Trelease.'

'Hello, Tom. What have you got there?'

He held out the trays. 'These are seedlings of a plant called Love-in-a-Mist — or *nigella* if you want its botanical name,' he said, then turned to me. 'But Jill, look at the colour of them.

Have you ever seen anything like it?'

I gazed at the small plants in amazement and felt my jaw drop. They had just begun flowering and through the hazy green bracts that were the 'mist', the blossoms were a beautiful shade of golden yellow. '*Yellow!*' I exclaimed as our eyes met. 'But . . . but . . . *nigella* are only ever pink, blue or white!'

'I know,' Tom said, as Bran looked curiously over his shoulder. 'That's what I mean. Isn't it interesting? Looks like you could have a whole new variety here. What do you think?' He gazed earnestly into my face as my mind whirled.

Judy and I had found the seed pods in the garden when we first arrived. Had they hybridised themselves by merging with another plant? Things like that did happen. And to discover, or to breed, a totally new variety was every gardener's dream.

'If only,' I said with a laugh, 'but I expect it's only a freak, a one-off. We can't be sure until we know if its seeds come true next time. But it's certainly amazing.'

'Anyway, I've got to go — I can hear Ginger calling me.' Tom thrust the trays of plants into my hands and turned away. 'We were in the middle of a two-handed job up in the poly-tunnel when I found these. I just had to show them to you.' He grinned and went loping back up the rising ground.

'Incredible!' I could hardly take my eyes off the little plants as I moved back into the potting shed to place them under the window in the maximum amount of light.

Bran took a closer look. 'What are you going to do about these, Jill?' He raised his head and faced me. 'I think you should tell the R.H.S. They'd be really interested, wouldn't they? They would verify them for you, too. What do you think?'

'The Royal Horticultural Society?' I frowned and nibbled a lip. 'But they're the national experts. I'd probably only be making a fool of myself. Anyway, their headquarters is somewhere way up country, isn't it?

'It's in Surrey. A place called Wisley.'

'But I couldn't leave things here to go traipsing off on what's probably only a wild goose chase.'

'But what if it isn't?' Bran said earnestly as our eyes met. 'Think about it, Jill. Your business would become famous. Nationally. Internationally even. You'd have growers and seed merchants from all over beating a path to your door. You could make a fortune.'

'And pigs'll fly first,' I retorted. 'No, Bran, there's no way I can possibly go.' I turned away.

'But I could.' The words fell into utter silence as I felt my jaw drop.

'Wh . . . what did you say?' I jerked back to him.

'I said *I* could go. You see, I'm due to attend the annual reunion of former students at the agricultural college I went to. That's in Guildford. Very near Wisley. So, I could go to the R.H.S.

while I'm up there.'

'You could?' I felt my eyes pop. 'You would do that . . . for *me*? B . . . but why? Why would you go to . . . all that trouble?'

Bran came fully into the shed and pulled the door closed behind him. Relieving me of the tray of plants, he carefully placed it on one side and, covering my hand with his own, gently pulled me closer.

'Jill,' he said tenderly, 'do you really not know?'

'Of course I don't.' I shook my head and gazed into his eyes. In the shadowy room they were huge, deep and compelling.

It was cosy and peaceful in the shed, the atmosphere smelling sweetly of compost, moist soil and ancient wood. Dust motes danced in the sunbeams striking through the dusty glass, as time stopped while Bran stepped forward, placed both arms around my shoulders and clasped me to him.

'Because I've loved you from the first

moment we met,' he whispered, his face against my hair, his warm breath on my cheek. Every bone in my body turned to jelly as the room tilted. If Bran had released me I would have fallen.

'Loved you and admired your courage. For being brave enough to give up everything to follow your dream. I've watched you struggle, working all hours, battling all winds and weathers. And wishing I could tell you how much you mean to me.' His grip tightened.

I tried to take it in. Bran *loved* me? I couldn't believe it. After all the anguish, the pain when I'd been so careful to hide what I felt for him, he'd loved me all the time? I raised my face, so close to his, and met that hypnotic gaze.

'But . . . but . . . you've never said, or hinted, or given me the least idea how you felt before. Why, Bran?'

'Oh, I've wanted to. You'll never know how much I've wanted to. But it's because — Jill, I have a child. I'm committed to bringing him up. I can't expect you to take Ricky on, especially after the time you told me you can't stand children. I know now that's not true, but . . . but today, now, I was just . . . overcome. I had to let you know how much I love you, even if you can never feel the same way about me. So now . . . ' He loosened his clasp and went to put me from him.

'Oh, Bran, no!' I would not let him go, but only clung the more tightly, alternately laughing and weeping as a storm of wild emotions I'd never felt before swept through me and I buried my face in his neck.

'You don't understand! I've loved you too, as far back as I can remember, but I couldn't show it, because I thought you didn't care for me! And I'm really fond of Ricky. How could I not be, when he's a part of you?'

Then his soft lips came down to mine and we lost ourselves in each other as time ceased to exist and life outside rolled on without us.

* * *

Bran went up to Surrey the next morning, taking a tray of my precious plants with him. He'd promised to ring me on his mobile as soon as he had been to Wisley, which he did a couple of evenings later.

'Jill, the guy I spoke to is really interested and he's going to contact you himself. He thinks it's pretty certain the plants are a new species — he's just got to check them out with his superiors. So I left the specimens with him, knowing you have some more. Have to go, darling; the signal's breaking up.'

''Darling!'' I sighed with contentment as I put down the receiver. How good that sounded. And the plants! I could hardly believe such happiness could exist. How my fortunes could change in such a short space of time. My life had become a waking dream.

Next time Bran called was to say he was home and on his way down to see me. Too excited to wait for him, I walked up through the field towards the farm. What a lot had happened here since we'd first met. My accident. Marie's treachery. Bran's upward swing from the pit of despair to his present euphoria. My amazing plants. And I imagined how thrilled Lorna would have been if she'd known what had turned up in her garden.

But most wonderful of all, of course, was our discovery of each other. Now each step was taking me nearer to the most important person in my life. And soon we would be together forever.

THE END